Join the resistance!

The Jericho Resistance Series:

A Rebel in Jericho

Twice Redeemed

The Fires of Faith

I0626138

You just made a difference!

Thank you for choosing this novel. Twenty percent of all proceeds goes to the fight against human trafficking.

What readers are saying about The Jericho
Resistance series:

"I felt it was a great read. The plot was interesting
and kept me turning the pages… I can't wait to
read more by this author!"

-    Carrie, *A Rebel in Jericho*

"The love story is great, but the suspense was
even better. There were times in the story I
absolutely could not put the book down!"

-    Christina L., *A Rebel in Jericho*

"Suspense, romance, deception, and the desire to
survive. I look forward to continuing this
series…"

-    Josh, *A Rebel in Jericho*

Twice Redeemed

The Jericho Resistance: Book Two

Mimi Milan

© 2016 by Michele Claudio

Cover by Kirk DouPonce
DogEared Design
www.dogeareddesign.com

Published by Eaton House
P.O. Box 19795
Charlotte, NC 28219-0795

ASIN: B01DL85L60

For speaking engagements, interviews, or other inquiries, please contact the author at:

writemimimilan@gmail.com
www.mimimilan.com
www.facebook.com/AuthorMimiMilan

Produced in the United States of America.

For my *suegra*,

Esperanza.

A Godlier woman I've never known.
Thank you for changing my life.

Did you know… ?

Painted ladies of the Wild West entered their profession for many different reasons. While some were attracted to the opportunity of making as much as ten dollars a week, others were simply born into the profession. Their mothers having been "working women," their own names were already tainted for any life other than that of a saloon girl.

However, it was not uncommon for a woman to become a red light lady because of necessity. Sometimes women were abandoned for various reasons (like when there became too many mouths to feed). Often, they were widowed due to unforeseen illness or incidents like shootouts. Therefore, becoming a soiled dove was a means of survival.

Unfortunately, some ladies became saloon workers through no choice of their own. Sad stories of women taken or sold against their will was not uncommon. Under the guise of protection, they would join caravans westward bound… only to unknowingly arrive at a cathouse. Meanwhile, others followed tradition or allowed economic circumstances to dictate the marriage of a daughter to a stranger. Things didn't always turn out as planned, though.

Twice Redeemed is the story of one such woman, struggling to survive in a southwestern border town by any means necessary.

Acknowledgments

As always, this book would not have been made possible without the help of so many wonderful individuals. I'd like to thank as many of you as possible, but space is limited. So I apologize if I miss anyone.

First and foremost, I give all praise to God for seeing me through another book. I hope this story inspires readers as much as I was inspired to write it.

Thank you to my husband for not only understanding, but accepting the quirks that come along with being married to a "weird writer." I could not have written this book without you.

Kirk DouPonce, you have done it again! Thank you for capturing Mercedes so well. You truly are a talented cover designer.

To my beta readers. Your input is invaluable and necessary. My books wouldn't be the same without your careful eyes and questioning minds. Thank you for reading the first drafts.

For all the kind readers out there who said something nice about my first novel, thank you so much! I hope you enjoy reading this book as much (or more) than the first, and that the rest of the series lives up to your expectations.

Thank you to the English faculties at the University of North Carolina at Charlotte and

Queens University. Their phenomenal instruction has strengthened my writing skills over the past few years.

To all the critique partners I've had over the past two years, I appreciate all the input you've given me. The feedback everyone has provided has been tremendous, and I wish all of you nothing but success.

Lastly, all my love to the family who have been a constant source of inspiration and support. You all helped build this brand of insanity! ☺

"For He rescued us from the domain of darkness, and transferred us to the kingdom of His beloved Son, in whom we have redemption, the forgiveness of sins."

- Colossians 1:13 – 14

Chapter One

Nogales, Sonora, Mexico – August 1918

"Por el amor de…"

Mercedes let out a slow breath, tracing the swollen flesh around her left eye with a gentle finger as she stared at her reflection in the cracked mirror. She couldn't remember who her assailant had been the night before since he wore a bandana, but she knew it had to be the same man who assaulted her three weeks prior because of the slur he used.

Malinche.

Traitor.

Just about every man who frequented the Jericho saloon treated her as such. It hadn't taken long for Belmonte's watchdogs to worm out a confession from one of the other girls. The resulting rage had her hair standing on end when he cursed; a chair flung across the parlor. He was beyond livid to find out she was the one to help that American girl, Catalina, escape. Of all the people to betray him, Mercedes was the least likely to do so. Sold to Belmonte at the innocent age of fifteen, she had spent the better part of a decade gaining his trust. Aside from La Fea, she was the only one permitted to roam the market, flitting from one *puesto* to another in search of food and other necessities to run his business. Now she was confined by the same four walls day in and day out.

And game for even the cruelest of customers.

Studying her face, she pulled out a small compact. The pale powder was a slight shade darker than the beige bedroom walls, but still much lighter than her own sun-kissed complexion.

"Perhaps that's a good thing." She mused under her breath, dabbing at the compressed dust. The lighter color may have been just what was needed to cover the purplish bruise; a dark crescent moon pinned on the rim of her delicate cheekbone.

The bell on the wall rang and she dropped the compact, the contents bursting into a fine cloud.

"La madre!"

Mercedes kneeled beside the make-up to pick up a few small clumps that remained. She stuck a ragged fingernail into the crack of a floorboard and fished out a larger piece when the bell chimed again.

What would happen if she cut the string connected to it? She could always lie and say the damage occurred the night she was attacked.

No, that wouldn't work. Cutting the thread would make the one that ran along the wall in the parlor loosen, or even fall. She would be the obvious culprit, punished for falling short once again.

A terse knock at the door shot her upright like a bullet.

"Ya voy!" She straightened her skirt, brushing off a mild dusting of powder from the black fabric. "I'll be down in a minute."

The heavy wooden door creaked open all the same. La Fea peeked into the room.

"Mercedes Angelina Nobles. Apúrate, nena!" She snapped her fingers at her friend. "You know el jefecito doesn't like to be kept waiting."

Mercedes smiled at the younger woman's feigned admiration for their owner. Although, gratitude wouldn't have been too far from truth for her friend. La Fea had arrived at Jericho when she was even younger than her own delicate age. Nine? Ten at most. A dirty little urchin that for some unknown reason Belmonte allowed to run around like some wild animal. The ladies all figured it was because she was a useless kid who had yet to learn how to please a man. What was his excuse now, though? He had permitted her the luxury of maturing into a grown woman who looked more like something that spent the days rolling around in the dirt, instead of a working woman in the only saloon littering the border town of Nogales. Truth be told, the girl proved such a fright that Mercedes wondered if she ever bathed. She knew that she must have, though.

Otherwise, the inevitable stench would have killed them all long ago.

Perhaps that would have been preferable to entertaining multiple *chivatos* night after night.

"A que ves?" La Fea jacked her chin up. "You like my face so much, maybe you should paint a picture."

Mercedes snorted and looked away, embarrassed that she had been caught staring – a bad habit becoming worse since the routine attacks. She just couldn't shake the evil feeling that someone was always watching; waiting.

"Sorry. Guess I got lost in my own little world." She waved the girl away, refusing to voice her thoughts out loud. La Fea was the only one to show her any sympathy after Belmonte found out the role she played in Catalina's getaway. A few medicinal herbs at the right time had sent most of his men in search of a place to relieve their stomachs. The incident at customs had directed the rest of them to the border, fearful that American soldiers were invading to take over their lands. "I'll be down in a minute."

She looked at herself in the mirror again and ran a hand down her figure, thankful that it was still slim.

La Fea threw her hands up.

"Ay, amiga! Everyone knows you look good." She paused and Mercedes looked up. The girl winked and pointed to her eye. "Even with that fat face you got."

Mercedes swatted at her friend who only giggled as she jumped back, then raced out the room. She chased after the girl, down the hall of painted adobe, colorful Aztecan gods looking down with disapproval until the pair skid to a stop at the edge of the stairs. They both knew Belmonte wouldn't tolerate anything less than complete subservience in the parlor. Their playful behavior would belie that image and his authority.

"Suerte." La Fea whispered under her breath as she veered off to the right, heading for the usual corner she hid in to embroider the cloth *servilletas* they used to keep the tortillas warm.

Mercedes repeated the hopeful wish, but was pretty certain that between the two of them, she was in much greater need of good luck. So much so that she had even taken to reading the Bible left behind by Catalina. Not that she believed any of it. She had given up on fairytales the day her parents prayed Belmonte would find her a good home.

She could still remember the two men negotiating. Her papá, desperate to get enough coin to never have to part with another child, looked like the frail *viejo* she soon realized he had always been. Belmonte, glorious like the golden calf that deceived Israel, argued down to the last *peso* with false promises of manna dripping off the tip of his slithering tongue.

And then there had been her mamá.

She could still feel the hot breath in her ear, a fervent prayer bequeathing her with all the blessings the Heavens could create. Then her mother pulled away and crossed her "hija tan preciosa," the woman's warm fingertips coming to rest a second time on her forehead before running them down her daughter's cheek.

"Mujer!"

Mercedes wiped the back of her hand across the good eye and pushed back her long, dark braid as she hustled up to the bar counter. Belmonte grabbed hold of her arm, yanking her close enough to smell the Yuerba buena he chewed.

"What took you so long, *woman*?" The steady rhythm of his jaw chomping on the minty herbs mesmerized her, and she wondered what would happen if a person were to straight-chew Senna. "First you undermine my authority. Then you keep my customers waiting. The food's getting cold, the beer's turning flat. Estás loca?"

He released her with a shove towards the counter where several new Talavera plates sat. Amorina, the latest girl to be acquired, spooned large portions of frijoles onto one of the clay pieces painted with a mariposa. The Monarch's wings spanned from edge to edge, a milky-white glaze forever trapping him.

"Buenas, floja."

Mercedes gritted her teeth, the sound echoing in her ears.

"It's not afternoon yet." She snatched up two readied plates. "And I'm not lazy."

"Close enough. You've spent most of the morning in your room like some *princesa* while the rest of us had to do your chores." Amorina slammed the large silver ladle down onto the counter, and made two firm fists. "You owe me for laundry duty!"

"Ni madres!" She dropped the plates back onto the counter, ready to claw at the hateful woman. "All you did was cry like a little *chillona* the first few weeks you got here. Who was doing your part then?"

"Que se callen!" Belmonte grabbed the ladle from the counter. Stepping between the two women, he raised it high in the air, ready to strike. "Both of you shut your mouths and get to work. Ahora!"

His growl sent them both scurrying away, Amorina whispering revenge under her breath.

"Suerte." Mercedes tossed back, the word laced with sarcasm as she walked around the counter. She leaned over, snatched the plates up again, and made her way towards a couple of ranch hands sitting in a lonely corner. She set the first plate in front of one man, a chivato who reminded her of a mean, old goat that spent most of its days roaming the ranch, searching to satisfy a hunger no woman could ever quench. He caught her looking at him, and she quickly averted her eyes.

"Señor." She nodded, her eyes still cast downward, and turned towards his companion. He looked like the kind of vaquero who spent more time chasing the calves than the bulls. Too soon to be put out to pasture; too old to keep up with the young bucks. She reached over to set down his food when she felt a swift strike from behind. The hard blow filled her cheeks with heat, and sent her flying into the cowboy. Food flung all over him. He jumped up and the beautiful Talavera crashed to the ground, a puzzle of broken pieces. Expletives filled his mouth as he brushed the food off.

"Mujer de basura!" He grabbed her by the braid and fire seared through her scalp. "Mi vieja just made me this shirt."

The other man stood. "Make that perra clean it up."

"Asi es." He yanked her head close, burying her face in his chest. "Use your tongue."

Her eye pushed in under the pressure of his firm grip. The tender flesh throbbed with renewed pain, and her eyes filled with tears.

She cried for help.

"YA BASTA!"

Mercedes felt the immediate sweet release of her hair as Belmonte approached them, four of his men crowding either side of him.

"You gonna' side with this Malinche after all she's done?"

The man's tone filled Mercedes with the realization that he had been her attacker. She backed away from him, hopeful Belmonte would offer some small salvation.

"Qué no!" He turned away from her with disgust, hocking a string of spit to the floor. "I wouldn't trust that bruja with a broom. She'd be liable to fly off on it instead of sweeping the floors."

"Then give her to us." The man ran his tongue across his top teeth. "We'll take real good care of her for you."

His threatening tone made Mercedes shutter. She edged closer to Belmonte.

"Por fa." She searched his face, begging him to please save her.

He only crossed his arms, disappointment clearly written all over his face. Then the man took another step forward, reaching out for Mercedes. Her breath caught in her chest, the feeling of immense weight pressing in on her as she fought to breathe again. She began to swoon.

"Stop." Belmonte held a hand up to the vaquero while one of his guards caught Mercedes and set her upright again. "This is MY cantina, and what I say goes. And what I say is that you have to 'pay to play.' But, hijole, you don't have the pesos."

Belmonte rubbed his thick fingers together, indicating that Mercedes was far above the man's pocket.

"How much for the Malinche?"

Belmonte paced the floor, stroking his chin as if in deep thought. She had seen this act before. In fact, it was the same tactic he used to purchase her from on her father. A cat and mouse game of take and release.

He would sell her if the price was right.

"One thousand pesos."

"¿Como?"

The man's jaw dropped open. Belmonte nodded his head as he approached the man and patted his shoulder. He turned him around and began walking him towards the front doors.

"Like I said, amigo, the price is too high."

"The price is crazy!" The man argued, but allowed himself to be escorted out. His older compadre followed.

"He's right, you know. I wouldn't pay that kind of money for a horse, let alone a traitorous woman."

Belmonte stepped aside and allowed the second man to pass. "Then you, my friend, don't know the price of a good horse."

"Maybe I don't, but I do know the price of a good woman." He thumbed back to Mercedes, casting a quick glance over his shoulder. "And that right there is no good woman. You need to teach her a lesson, *my friend*, or someone else is gonna' do it for you."

The look on Belmonte's face revealed his understanding of the subtle threat.

"Don't worry." His hand reached for his pistol. He fingered the butt of it. "She gonna' get her lesson."

Would he really shoot her?

The man looked over at Mercedes once more, then nodded at Belmonte and turned on his heel.

She watched the patron make his way across the street for a moment, thankful that the pair had finally left. She wasn't sure what Belmonte would do, but she knew he would hold true to his words. If he didn't, then he'd have a bigger fire to put out later when other men came searching for her, determined to teach her a lesson for selling out her own kind. They would get their pound of flesh one way or another.

"Ay, mujer." Belmonte kept his back turned towards her, but she could sense his irritation. "Mujer, mujer."

"I'm sorry." She feared the apology wouldn't suffice this time, having whispered it a dozen times since the incident. "I can make it up to you."

She approached him, slow but sure. This was the one thing she knew she was good at. She reached out and placed a hand on his shoulder, softly massaging it with the hope that he would turn to face her. One kiss and he'd be hers. Then he would forget the whole thing.

At least, for a little while.

She felt the tension begin to release, and his back slumped. She stepped closer, almost close enough for their bodies to touch. He reached up and wrapped his hand over hers, guiding it to a different spot to massage.

"See?" She whispered into his ear, low and soft. "I can make it better."

She felt his deep inhale; heard his long, quiet sigh. He gave her hand a gentle squeeze.

Then his grip grew.

"I really wish you could, amor." He turned, still holding her hand. Then he pulled her arm up, bending it backwards as he crushed her small palm with his fist. She cried in protest, but he kept twisting her limb and forced her back towards the counter where Amorina worked.

The girl dropped the utensils she was using to prepare plates of food, a look of horror painted on her face. She backed away from the pair.

Mercedes felt the owner's full weight as he bore down, pressing her hard against the counter. He reached past her to one of the plates and picked up a carving knife.

She struggled beneath him. "Please! Please don't."

He grabbed her by the hair, willing her to stand still. Fire seared through her skull once more. He pointed the knife at her, the sharp blade flashing in her face as he spoke.

"Ya, cállate!"

Her scream filled the bar as he brought the knife down and began to saw away.

Chapter Two

"Ain't nothing to declare coz I ain't brought nothing back yet." John Durbin shifted in his saddle, refusing to dismount. It was almost midday and he was eager to get across the border and on with his mission. Why were soldiers working the border crossing anyway? A couple of wet-behind-the-ear young guns. What were they? Eighteen at best? John frowned at the idea of answering to someone half his age and with even less experience. And wasn't this a job for the customs agents anyway?

"Didn't know you boys stopped people from going out. Thought it was more an issue of what's coming in."

"That used to be the case, sir." The boy soldier pulled out a small packet of chewing tobacco. He stuck a small clump of it under his bottom lip before offering it to his comrade, then spoke again. "Things have changed a bit since that little incident we had a while back."

John nodded grimly. "Little incident" didn't even begin to cover it. One of the soldiers had taken a potshot at an unarmed Mexican returning home to his family when he failed to stop at customs. Had everyone up in arms.

Literally. The Mexicans saw their fellow countryman fall to the ground, and everyone ran to get their rifles to defend themselves from Americans invading their lands. Meanwhile, the soldiers heard the shots and thought the Germans had paired up with Mexico to invade the United States. Next thing anyone knew, it was an all-out battle between the two towns.

Just a downright mess!

"So you boys are looking for deserters?"

"No, sir." The young man offered the pouch up to John who only waved it away. He looked uncomfortably at his comrade who only shrugged. He pocketed the rest of the tobacco and leaned in, lowering his voice as if sharing a secret. "We're looking for spies. You know, anyone trying to pass supplies to aid the Mexicans."

"Yeah!" His friend chimed in. "Just in case we was right, and them Germans plan on coming up through ol' Mexico."

John let out a quiet sigh. Who would have ever thought that political affairs from so far away could have such an impact on his own country? It wasn't like anyone had declared war on American soil. Yet troops had been recruited and trained; the majority of them shipped out while the rest of these boys were forced to sit and stew. Most days ended with news of another fallen friend, dying on foreign grounds too cold to care for a proper burial. They were aching for a fight, and dredging up old hurts regarding that invisible border line would do just fine for now.

He could have schooled them about the ignorance of it all – that whole "die by the sword" dictum. But his Pappy hadn't raised no preacher man, and knowing a few scriptures didn't make him one neither. No, sir. He had his own battles to fight, and debts to repay.

"Well, it's like I said earlier." John tipped his Stetson, his voice holding the kind of authority that had been useful during his sheriffing days. He tapped his heels into Abigail's side, urging the horse forward. "Ain't nothing to declare."

The first soldier raised his hand and reached up to grab Abigail's chinstrap. The horse jerked away.

"Whoa. Easy, son." John chided the younger. Didn't he know better than to touch another man's horse? "She's a little head shy. Liable to buck up and trample a stranger for touching her without invite."

"Kind of like a woman."

John snorted at the crude comparison, but couldn't contradict fact.

"Alright, then." The soldier stood a little taller. His voice grew serious. "What business have you got over there anyway?"

John debated on how to answer for a moment. How apt were they to understand that he had intentions of helping a Mexican who once helped him?

He decided to keep it simple. "A woman."

Both boys snickered, then the first stepped aside and waved him pass.

"Enjoy the conquest."

He ignored the flippant remark and made his way across International Boulevard where he was inspected once again, but this time by two Mexicans hesitant to let him through. He waved a wad of dollar bills at them. They took it, counting the money. Signaling their approval when they were done, John continued down the dirt road. Adobe houses painted the landscape on either side, mostly white and dingy from days of dust and lack of rain. He took note of the ones that stood out. A rare, fiery orange that his younger eyes had often seen in the setting sun of New Mexico; a blue that could only exist where the sea meets the white sands of a faraway island in some children's book.

The townspeople dotted the street, some in front of their rustic homes as they completed one chore or another. Others had set up makeshift puestos. A robust woman in front of a modest abode with a wooden cross above the door, swept her steps with enough fervor to remove the devil had he the insolence to show. Another stood opposite a stand, calling to any passerby who would take notice of the various clay pots or woven blankets featuring slaughtered braves from centuries ago.

John dismounted his horse and an elderly woman limped towards him with a saddle blanket. She began rattling off in Spanish as she held the item up. He shook his head that he wasn't interested, and tried asking where the church was instead.

"*Casa de Dios?*" House of God was about as good as he was going to get. He brought his hands up, a triangular point that he hoped she would understand as a roof. Then he made a cross with his two index fingers.

The old woman hesitated.

"Iglesia?"

"That's right!" He gave her a big grin when he recognized the word for church and nodded. "*Si, si. Iglesia, por favor.*"

The woman smiled back but only stood there. John stared at her in awkward confusion. Hadn't he just requested that she show him where to find the church? At least, he believed he had. Maybe his Spanish needed even more work than he thought. He studied the woman for a moment, giving her a once over. That's when he caught the small, feeble hand protruding from behind her revolso.

"Oh." John dug into his pocket and pulled out a couple of dollar bills. He figured he better be a little generous. Otherwise, he would end up God only knew where, probably in the middle of the desert.

Or worse!

The old crone accepted the money, her hand quickly pulling back behind the shawl the moment she grasped the bills. She motioned excitedly for him to follow her, and John held on tight to Abigail as he led her down the street. They turned a corner and she stopped, pointing out across the center square.

She charged me to walk down the street?

John fixed his face, knowing the expression was the same don't-pull-nothing-funny brow raise he had used during his sheriffing days. The woman feigned innocence, lifting her hands as if surprised herself that the church stood where it did.

"What?" She asked.

He could feel heat climb the back of his neck and race up the sides of his face. He sputtered. "You — you speak English! Why didn't you say so?"

She smiled, her accent thick. "You didn't ask."

John just let out a sigh, and waving her away, watched the woman limp back down the dirt road, a low chuckle indicating she had won the upper hand. He shook his head, deciding that the viejita probably saw more sorrow in a week's time than he had his entire life, and the blessed bills would undoubtedly feed her for at least that long.

Facing front again, he surveyed the stately building. It was simple like most of the adobe creations surrounding him, but projected a sense of protection. Rectangular and white, sunlight bounced off the walls and made the parish glow with the illusion that the pearly whites of Heaven had sprung up as a safe haven amidst the growing corruption of Nogales. However, the wooden cross affixed above the door paled in comparison to a single stain glassed window, dust on the sill indicating its recent installation. John approached it and studied the picture, recognizing it as the Mexican version of the mother of Christ. The virgin of Guadalupe. She looked down at him, mercy and understanding depicted in her eyes despite the obvious neglect she suffered. Compelled, he reached up and wiped away some of the grime that her robes had collected, and brushed away the powder from beneath her feet. Then he turned back and approached the door, nervous to leave his horse unattended but eager to find the priest that could possibly put him up for the night.

That is, put *them* up for the night. Surely a man of the cloth wouldn't reject John's plan just because the woman involved was a working girl. Would he?

He grabbed ahold of the handle, ready to pull on it when the door swung open. Across from him stood a man in liturgical garments, a crimson ferraiolo over a flowing black cassock. Seeing such elegance took John by surprise. Before leaving the States, his friends had impressed upon him that he would be dealing with a simple servant of God. However, the formidable gentleman filling out the space of the door appeared to be of some rank.

"Father Emmanuel?" He noted the mistrusting tone of his own voice and cleared his throat.

The man on the other side of the threshold looked him over once, and apparently determining him to be of some worth, stepped aside. "No, but do come in, my son." He showed him into the foyer.

John removed his hat, knocking it against the side of his leg to brush off some of the dirt before entering. He examined his surroundings, the bright white walls smooth and oblique and melting into an arch that separated the narthex from the nave. He stopped before entering the holy room and, noting a small bowl of water atop a simple cement pillar, dipped his fingers into the vessel and combed them through his hair. The priest gave him a disdained look, and he deducted that his deed must have been blasphemous.

He tried to reconcile the situation.

"I'm sorry if I disturbed you, but some friends of mine told me that I could find a certain priest here by the name of Father Emmanuel."

The clergyman paused.

"I'm afraid you wasted your time coming here." He spoke catatonically. "Father Emmanuel is no longer in service of the church."

"Why not?"

A strange, disturbing smile formed on the man's face.

"Excommunicated, I'm afraid." He gave him another once over before further explaining. "How do you Americans say? Tossed out? Cut off? Well, I'm sure you get my meaning. He's no longer with us, and I am now tending to the flock of this parish."

The news was so surprising that it actually made John take a step back. He wasn't use to the kind of Christianity that severed ties between man and God. His own brand of worship was a direct line to "the man upstairs." And he couldn't even being to imagine someone having authority over that relationship.

Also, he couldn't envision this man "tending" to *anything*, leaving him to debate the idea of sharing his predicament with him. He decided better against it.

"And I'm guessing you wouldn't know where I could find this Father Emmanuel?"

"I could not," the man responded emphatically.

John made a small nod and slapped his hat back on his head. He tried to cover the sarcasm in his voice, only mildly succeeding. "Then in that case, I'll wish you a good day. *Padre*."

He touched the brim of his hat in acknowledgment, and the priest stepped forward. John raised a hand to stop him.

"I can see myself out." He turned on a boot.

"Indeed." The priest called after him with a tinge of mockery on the tip of his tongue. "Vaya con Dios."

John ignored him, seeing little gain from declaring that he always went with God.

There's no point in dallying any longer.

Thinking about the questionable priest, John knew he'd find little help there. The best thing he could do was search for someone willing to let out a room. Surely there would be any number of people eager to earn a couple of bucks.

That little old woman! She had made a play on his purse before. Surely she'd like a second helping.

He untied his horse and made his way down the street, looking this way and that. Finally coming upon the small puesto of ponchos and blankets, he found the woman packing up the goods.

Deciding her broken English to be better than his minimal Spanish, John spoke in his own native tongue. "Finished for the day?"

The old woman looked up, startled. "Why you come back? Money all gone."

"Really?" John found the possibility unlikely, but thought it would be disrespectful to accuse her of lying. For fact, she was still his elder – old enough to be his mammy had he ever had one. He turned a pleasant tone, one he thought he'd have used on a loving mother. "Well, how's you'd like to get you a couple of dollars more?"

The woman raised a suspicious brow and scoffed. "What do you think I am? Dumb or something?"

"On the contrary! I think you're a smart ol' gal who knows a good deal when she hears one."

John slid up to the woman, his hand already pulling out the wad of cash. He began counting out a few bills. "I just need a room to stay for the night. I promise I'll be gone come tomorrow."

The woman's eyes were wide as she looked at his offering. She hesitated.

"Why you in Mexico?"

Did he tell her the truth? Could he confide in this woman? He studied her for a moment, her eyes hard with doubt. He gave her the bare essentials about his intentions, and the woman's eyes grew soft with kindness.

"You is red as the Devil." She wagged a finger at his mustache, then picked up a blanket and stuffed it in a burlap sack. "But he never pays American dollars. Help pack. Then I show you to a room."

John ran a hand over his face, deciding a close shave might make him a little less noticeable.

"Any chance the room comes with a razor?"

"Sí, señor." A small, sly smile formed. "It cost a peso to rent. But I give it to you, and the hot water and even the shaving crema for only one dollar more."

John shook his head, but laughed and reached into his pocket. He counted out one more bill and handed it over. "You drive a hard bargain."

She accepted the money and after tucking it somewhere beneath her revolso, lifted a burlap sack which she promptly handed over for him to carry. She picked up the second one and turned to leave. "So what they call you?"

"John. And you might be?"

"Doña Maria. No forget, eh? *Doña*."

"Yes, ma'am."

John acknowledged the term of respect and followed her into a house behind the fabric stand. He was shown his room and quickly informed that she kept a lock on her own, which would have insulted him had he not thought the better of it.

"Yes, ma'am," he repeated.

She disappeared and returned in no time with a small metal pail of water which was more lukewarm than hot, and slightly tinted blue. He guessed that the water had been drawn from whatever tub she used to dye her blankets. He must have worn a wary look because she said, "no pasa nada," and he silently questioned if that were true as she poured the water into the washbowl and set down a tiny container of grease that smelled like day old drippings.

"Better than la crema," she pointed at the jar with satisfaction. She limped away again, and John noticed the swollen leg she walked on.

"Thank you, ma'am." It was all he could think to say. He turned to the razor. There was no telling if anyone at the Jericho saloon would recognize him, but the possibility was more likely if he didn't shave. Sure as sin on a Saturday night, there couldn't have been too many men running around with Hellfire on their faces.

He took a gander at the mirror above the cooling bowl of blue water, trying to picture himself without the mustache. He cringed at the image he conjured up, but scooped up the grease all the same.

Chapter Three

Mercedes lifted her face to the scorching sun, a soft breeze brushing against one heated cheek. It did little to cool her. Cursing the hot day, she clenched her skirt tight with one hand. The freshly picked cilantro wafted up from within the folds of the fabric, clearing her senses. She tucked away the small paring knife she used to garden with inside a skirt pocket. Then she reached up to the bandana on her head.

"Te van a ver," La Fea called from the laundry line.

"I don't care if they see me," she retorted. She ripped the makeshift bandana off, exposing the bush of small curls that awkwardly framed her face. "No tengo la culpa que parezco asi!"

She used the wrap to wipe sweat from her face, then threw it to the ground.

"No, it's not your fault you look like that." La Fea took another wet bedsheet from the basket and flung it onto the line. "Although, it will become your fault if no one wants you tonight because they see you looking like that."

Mercedes cringed. Of all the rotten luck in the world, her pathetic situation wouldn't excuse her from entertaining whatever patrons Belmonte set up for her that evening. Wasn't it enough that he subjected her to some of the vilest of men? Did he have to go and chop off all her precious hair?

She felt her lips tremble, but she stiffened. Unsuccessful, a sob escaped before she could catch it.

"Ya, nena." La Fea called out to her. "Don't cry. It'll grow back soon."

Mercedes refused to answer. What did the girl know anyway? That's all she really was if truth be told. Sure, she had to slave away in the saloon like the rest of the women. However, she was never forced into the arms of one drunken dog after another, night after night.

Bitter disgust rose as bile in the back of her throat. She squeezed her eyes hard, hands clenching down on the herbs in her gathered skirts, and willed herself to calm down. It wasn't La Fea's fault that Belmonte didn't find the girl worthy enough to sell. If anything, Mercedes should be happy her friend was safe from the unwanted attention of such revolting men.

She let out a slow breath, her eyes slowly opening and focusing on the town beyond the iron gates. The church stood, shining like a promise for all the pure townspeople.

Pure.

A pang of disappointment surged through her, and she longed to be with the people on the outside of Jericho. To be *one* of them. But why? She had never felt that way before. Oh, she had always wished to be something other than a saloon girl serving whatever horrible order Belmonte threw her way. She got by well enough, though. At least she had until that Catalina girl arrived at Jericho, causing her to risk a neatly ordered world with talk of escape and God.

Was that it? There had been something different about Catalina. Something Mercedes originally wrote off as an American trait. Stories of how things were grander in America, where freedom was within grasp for those willing to take it. However, Catalina's talk of God stirred up the notion that her strength hailed from a source greater than that of her birthplace. How could that be, though? She had always held little concern for spiritual matters. She placed her faith in the everyday courtesies that graced her path. The gentleman who wanted nothing more than to casually discuss day-to-day musings. The girl from down the hall who was willing to scrub the laundry beside her.

She glanced back up at La Fea with a new batch of soiled laundry. The girl silently worked suds into what appeared to be a soldier's uniform. The horrible war was overseas, yet plenty of soldiers protected the southern borders just in case something went wrong.

It had, too.

Instead of allowing customs to do their job, the soldiers had stepped in and shot at a Mexican merchant returning home to his family. The gunfire had alerted the entire town. Fearful they were under attack, men from each household had grabbed a hold of their rifles and joined in shooting back. Little loss came of it other than the increasingly mistrustful relationship between the two countries.

Ay, sí. The American dog, too.

The short-lived battle had gone on long enough for Catalina to escape her abductor with a couple of her friends.

John Durbin.

She was picking herbs from the garden when a cowboy had come around looking for his friends. The sincerity in his voice had won her over immediately. Right away she knew that she wanted to help the man regardless of the risks. So they hatched a plan, and she brewed a cold sweet senna tea for Belmonte's watchmen while John went off for the horses. It wasn't long for the herb to take effect, and the men were sent scurrying away with stomach cramps in search of a place to relieve themselves.

Then came the coincidental gunfire from across the border.

Coincidental, or divine providence?

Mercedes remembered John saying those words, the dark green of his eyes jarring her almost as thoroughly as they did the last time she saw them. When he had stretched out his hand from atop his horse, asking her to ride away with him. But fear had clenched her heart, paralyzing her to leave Jericho and the life she had grown accustomed to.

Remorseful tears filled her eyes. She turned from the gate, refusing to think about the lost possibility of escape.

She glanced back up at La Fea and the bucket of hot suds, lost in the steam that spiraled upwards, belying the sweltering temperatures of the day's heat.

Reluctant to step in and help, Mercedes glanced away, stealing one last glance at the now forbidden town and its people who lived free. Taking a step back towards the suffocating saloon, she paused and studied the figure of a man on the horizon. For some unknown reason, he demanded her attention. There was something familiar about his long, confident gait that shifted almost in unison with the horse that trailed behind him. Mercedes studied the sleek brown mare strutting down the road, majestic in structure.

There was no forgetting that horse!

John?

Mercedes squeezed her eyes shut, chasing back the figment, then opened them again. Excitement bubbled up inside her. How many nights had she spent thinking about him, wishing he would return and again ask her to ride off? The brief encounter had been enough to fill her with fascination. She thought back to that day. The intensity in his eyes, the sincerity of his voice as he searched for his friends. The silent confidence that he would find them. He was the knight in shining armor her mother had talked about in bedtime stories to her and her siblings. Faded memories of her family came to mind, but she pushed them back to focus on John. Yes, it was him. She could never forget him...

Or his fiery red whiskers.

Mercedes studied him as he continued walking. He was almost close enough to actually determine his features, when she realized the startling fact that he had shaved off his brilliant moustache. The smallest twang of lament touched her, but she quickly brushed it aside. No matter. A person's hair wasn't what made an individual.

Hair!

Mercedes stiffened, hands flying up to her head. The contents from her skirts scattered along the ground as her fingers landing in a mass of dark ringlets. What in the world would he think at the sight of her? Would he turn in disgust? What if he thought of her like all the other men did? Ugly and worthless. No, surely someone who would risk his own life to rescue his friends wouldn't be that petty. Still, panic set in. She couldn't let him see her like this! She rushed away from the gate.

"*Qué pasó?*" La Fea looked up, sharp with concern. "You look like you ate too many tamales."

"Remember the American cowboy I told you about?" Mercedes began pacing back and forth. "The sheriff looking for Catalina?"

"Yeah. So?"

"He's coming up International."

La Fea glanced up and at the boulevard that separated the town from its American counterpart. Delight painted her face.

"That's wonderful!"

"No, it's not!" Mercedes let out a desperate cry. "Look at me!"

She stooped down, snatching up the bandana from the ground. She slapped it against her side, a small dust cloud puffing off it. The she quickly wrapped it around her head, fingers fumbling to tie a knot at the nape of her neck. "What if he finds out, and blames me?"

La Fea's face puckered at the sour thought. "Ay, amiga. I hate it when you speak in riddles. Why would he blame you?"

"Don't you get it?" Mercedes covered her face as if she could hide the shame welling up inside. She looked back up at her friend, the tone of her voice rising along with the despair she felt. "He offered me a way out, and I chose to stay. Now my face is bruised, my hair is gone… and let's not forget the *other* thing that happened. One look at me, and he'll think I'm worse than foolish for staying behind!"

She squeezed her eyes shut, hot tears forming behind her closed lids. A gentle hand touched her arm. She looked up into La Fea's determined face.

"We can't do much more than powder your face, but we can hide the other issues easy enough."

"How?"

"Well, first of all, don't go saying anything about the attack. I'm sure nothing will come of that. The hair is an easy fix, too. We just need to find some to borrow."

"What?" Mercedes gave the girl a look of disbelief. They had heard stories from abroad of girls selling their hair, but it was highly unlikely that a Mexicana would be willing to part with her long locks. "Girl, listen. You are sadly mistaken if you think one of these *sucias* is going to help us out. Not a single one would cut off an inch to save her own mother."

"Chica, please. We won't even need to ask one of the girls." La Fea kicked at the pile of dirty clothes on the ground beside her. "Let's leave the laundry for later, and go clean out the stalls."

Mercedes thought on the suggestion for a moment. A small glimmer of hope burned inside her when she realized what her friend was suggesting.

"No! You don't mean—"

"Uh, huh. Eso es."

Mercedes grabbed a hold of the girl, pulling her into a tight embrace. "You're brilliant. Do you know that?"

"Of course!"

Both girls laughed for a moment, then the seriousness of the situation set upon them. They took off, racing through the yard towards the southwest wall that divided the back of the property in two. They entered an adobe corridor of crumbling walls leading to the horse stables and corral. The flaking red earth belied of anything beautiful beyond them, and it was true as far as the stables themselves were concerned. Old, rotting planks and rusted nails formed the stalls and shed. Used ropes, darkened with the sweat and grime of too many hands, hung on the walls. However, the four horses that Belmonte kept were all healthy and whole.

"That one!" La Fea pointed at the last stall to a brown Criollo.

Mercedes screwed up her nose a bit. "Do you really think so?" She approached the horse, and stretched a hand out to touch his mane. It was softer than she thought it would be, but not more so than her own. "His hair is a bit coarse."

"It's just for looks." La Fea stepped forward and unlatched the stall's door. "It's not like he's going to be running his hands through your hair or something."

She paused, a mischievous grin stretching across her face.

"At least, not right away."

"Ay, nena." Mercedes rolled her eyes. "For someone who is supposed to be innocent, you sure do have a wicked mind."

"No. I just hope I find the right person in the right place once day."

"Well, help me pull this off and I'll send one to come get you."

La Fea snorted. "If you say so. Now give me something to cut with."

Mercedes looked around the stall for a moment, wondering what she could use when she remembered the paring knife. She dug into her skirt and produced it.

"It'll take a bit, but will go faster if you hold the hair tight while I cut." La Fea did as instructed and, within a matter of minutes, Mercedes had a fine handful of strands. "This should be enough to make a small braid. Come on. Let's go!"

She tucked the knife away just as a figure rounded the corner.

"What are you two doing in here?"

Amorina's sudden appearance startled both women, and Mercedes nearly dropped the hair. She quickly straightened, her grasp around the strands tightening.

"I suppose we could ask the same of you."

Amorina crossed her arms, clearly irritated. "Actually, I was sent to find *you*."

"Para?"

"Why do you think?" Amorina rolled her eyes before turning away. "You have an admirer."

She stalked off, mocking laughter filling the air.

"Don't worry about her." La Fea urged. "Just hurry up and make the braid."

Fingers trembling, Mercedes took a few strands of hair and tied them around the end of the others to form a bundle.

"Here. Hold this."

She held out the tied end for La Fea, then began separating the hair into three sections, loosely braided them together. She knotted the tail, then held the braid up for inspection.

"How does it look?"

La Fea plucked it up. "It'll do. Now turn around."

Mercedes helped her push part of the braid under the bandana. The end of it hung loosely behind her. She adjusted the wrap to cover her ears. Turning back to her friend, she embraced her once again.

"Gracias, amiga."

"Ya, ya." La Fea waved her off. "Go get your man before Amorina does."

The thought of Amorina digging her claws into someone like John sent Mercedes out of the stalls and back down the corridor. She raced through the yard as if fire lapped at her heels, stopping at the back entrance only long enough to straighten her skirt and check her braid once more. It was still tightly secured beneath the bandana.

Mercedes took a deep breath to steady herself. She glanced heavenward, a hopeful prayer nearly slipping from her lips. She bit her bottom lip, swallowing the words before they could escape.

Fairytales and "make believe" were for children.

Chapter Four

Silence settled over the bar as though death itself had paid a visit. John shifted, a bit hesitant but knowing it was too late to turn around. Besides, did he really want to? He had come with a purpose in mind, and wasn't the sort to turn tail and run just because the going looked a little tough. He scanned the bar, fixing a scowl on his face when he spotted a couple of American soldiers in a corner table. One had a heavily made up woman draped over him, pointing to a card he should play. Another comrade had a younger gal sitting on his lap, whispering into his ear. John could only imagine the message relayed by the shameless grin that overtook the man's face.

The soldier looked up, catching John's eye. He only touched the brim of his hat and made his way to the counter.

"Got anything other than beer or tequila?" John forewent any customary greeting, knowing it was better to look tough than friendly.

The portly bartender raised a brow, and John wondered if his attempt to avoid alcohol had just undone any display of machismo.

"Young pulque," the man responded.

Hoping the drink would be something tolerable, John nodded and watched as the bartender pulled out a pitcher. The man poured a thin, milky white liquid into a clay mug and pushed it forward.

"*Gracias, amigo.*" John brought the cup to his lips, and allowed the sweet mixture to momentarily linger on his tongue. He smiled at the barkeep. "Hey, now. This is pretty good!"

The man smiled back, a slightly rotted, half-toothless grin eliciting enough shock to make him laugh before wandering off to another patron. John took to a barstool with the intent of studying his surroundings a little better, but the touch of a soft hand on his shoulder turned his attention.

"You looking for a friend?" A young, heavily made up woman slowly ran her hand down his chest. Her accent was thick with suggestion. "I can be very good friend for you."

"Um, excuse me." John cleared his throat and lifted her hand off his chest. He gently released her, wondering how to refuse her without looking suspicious. "Not that you aren't beautiful and all, but I'm looking for a lady who can do something special."

The girl smiled knowingly. "Oh, I know very *special* things. What you looking for?"

Sigh. She really was young and beautiful. He hated the idea of hurting her feelings. However, truth be told, he didn't have the time nor patience for this kind of nonsense. All he really wanted was to get Mercedes and get on out of Jericho.

"Got any learning on herbal remedies? Making medicines?"

The girl's face fell flat. "No. Only the old lady know that." She thumbed behind her, and John looked up to see Mercedes staring at him from across the room. He could feel the beginnings of a smile tugging at the corners of his mouth. Inexplicable excitement bubbled up within, almost enough to lift him right off his stool. But then she glanced away to the man walking towards her and saw the discoloration of her face.

Heaven help the swine who had touched her. If he *ever* found out who the coward was, he'd —

"She for *special* party tonight."

"What?" John snapped his head back to the girl, disturbed. He looked at Mercedes again. The stranger had joined her, and leaned close to whisper something in her ear. He took hold of her hand, pulling her away from the crowded bar towards the staircase. Still, her dark eyes remained locked onto John. The misery he saw in them hit him hard, and he couldn't stop his gut reaction.

Swinging around and off the barstool, John crossed the room with a few quick strides. He placed himself in the man's path, a formidable barrier between Mercedes and whatever possibilities waited for her upstairs.

"Howdy, friend." There was nothing friendly in the tone of his voice, though, nor his stance. "I'd like to have a word with that woman, if you don't mind."

The stranger looked John over, but was relieved of having to react when another man spoke.

"Amigo, hello. Is there a problem I can fix for you?"

John looked past the stranger who still held firmly onto Mercedes, and studied the man who stood directly behind him. He was flanked on either side by men who looked ready to chew nails.

Belmonte.

John recounted Catalina's story about her abductors. This *had* to be the saloon owner. Short and portly, he sported a shaggy mustache that left the impression of an old, overfed dog. Harmless. The soulless look in his eyes declared he was anything but.

"Nah. We're good. I'm sure this gentleman and I can sort it out."

"Well, that's not exactly your call because this is my cantina." Two men stood and joined the owner. "Soy Belmonte, and I have the last say about who does what with my girls." John studied the two men flanking either side of the owner. He forged forward with the only explanation that came to mind.

"Well, that *señorita* over there said this was the one I wanted." John hoped he wasn't causing problems for the girl he pointed out.

"Oh, did she?" Belmonte smiled, but it looked anything other than pleasant. He waved the girl over. "Venga."

A look of panic marred her pretty features. She hesitated only a moment, though. Eyes cast down, she bravely approached Belmonte until she was within arm's reach. Then his hand shot out, latching onto her face.

"Look, mister. That ain't necessary." John quickly explained. "I simply asked a few questions and she answered them. That's how I knew which girl I was looking for."

Belmonte held on for a few seconds longer, then released the girl with a shove. "Well, it's like I said, amigo. She's already spoken for." He turned in a circle, arms spread out wide. The stumble in his step made it obvious that he was drunk. "But, look. I've got plenty of other girls to choose from. Younger, prettier. Trust me. You don't want that one anyway. She's hardly fit for a dog."

John swallowed hard, forcing himself to suppress a rebuttal. He had known any number of unpleasant chaps in his life. Shoo! Even rode with a few during his impressionable years, a time he liked to chalk up to being young and dumb. But even the biggest hothead in the group couldn't compare to the man standing in front of him now.

Maybe he could convince him. It would just depend on what kind of man Belmonte was when he drank. "Well, sir, that just might be the case. Then again, it might not. From my understanding, this gal is the only one in the place who knows a thing or two about plants. Might be able to help cure someone."

Belmonte's head swayed to Mercedes, his eyes squinting as he studied her. He turned back to John. "So your interest in her is not so much pleasure, but business?"

"That's right."

"Well, I like business. Business makes money." Belmonte gave him a skeptical look. "But I don't know if I believe you. Who is this person you say needs curing? Why don't you bring him here to do it?"

"Well, that's the thing. The 'he' is a 'she.' So I'm sure you can see why isn't with me now."

Belmonte's eyes narrowed. "Someone like you? An American woman? What does she look like?"

The sharp rise in the man's voice and John knew he had thought of Catalina. John hesitated. She was the last person he wanted to be connected to at a time like this!

"No, sir. She isn't American. I'm looking for help for a Mexican woman who lives right here in town."

"Which one? I know everyone in this town, and I haven't heard of any illnesses going around."

He paused. What if he said the wrong thing? What if Belmonte didn't care? The idea to verbally persuade Belmonte into letting Mercedes out of his sight was looking like a bad one. Perhaps he should have just gone with his instinct, and busted her out like he originally planned.

"You hear of Doña Maria?"

"Claro que sí." Belmonte smiled. "She has the best blankets in town. I have several for my horses. Finest ones around." His smile faded. "Why, what is wrong with her? She still have trouble with the leg?"

"Uh, yeah. That's exactly it."

"Ay, caray! I told the vieja to come here and have Mercedes look at it." Belmonte shrugged as if he suddenly realized it was no longer his problem. "What can I say? She refused. Said she could take care of it herself."

He turned as if the conversation was over.

"Well, it's obvious she couldn't." John tried approaching Belmonte, but took a step back when the men flanking either side of their boss stepped forward. "I'm just saying that you should see the leg. Looks meaner than a hog in heat, and that's a fair mean sight."

Belmonte laughed. "I've never heard it said like that. I'll have to remember it." He grew serious again. "But why do *you* care to help her? What's she to you?"

"Nothing except that I owe her. She's been real kind to me. Gave me a place to stay is all. Last thing I'd want is for her to up and die from some infection while I'm staying under her roof."

That much was true. No reason to explain why he was staying there.

He watched Belmonte begin to pace, the feeling of eternity settling in even though little more than a minute could have actually passed.

"I suppose it would do well to help her. She's one of the few useful people in this town."

One of guards stepped forward, whispering something low and fast in Spanish. John didn't understand every word, but he knew enough to pick up on the gist of it all. Being kind to the old woman would bode well for Belmonte in the eyes of the townsfolk. It would be proof that he was a benefactor of sorts, and they'd give him less grief about the business he ran within the walls of Jericho.

"Esta bien." He waved the man off, but addressed John. "You can take her to help the woman, but some conditions must be met. First, you have to pay this gentleman what he paid me, because you are taking his woman."

John wanted to ask why the man couldn't just have another girl, but stopped himself. The idea of *any* woman having to perform favors in exchange for money left a sour taste in his mouth. He nodded his consent and reached into his pocket.

"How much was that?"

"One thousand pesos."

"WHAT?!" John balked at the price. It was almost as much as a hundred bucks in American money. "I ain't never heard of such a thing."

Belmonte shrugged it off. "What can I say? I gave him something of a challenge. He was able to meet it."

John could feel the heat rising up his neck, and could imagine he looked as red as the fiery hair on his head. He bit the inside of his cheek to keep his temper in check. "Now, listen, partner. I ain't got that kind of money to give you." Belmonte waved him away. "But maybe I've got something even better."

The man paused. "Go on. I'm listening."

"You said you like horses. Right?" The man slowly bobbed his head. John rushed on. "Well, ain't nobody got a horse like my Abigail. She's a real beauty. Strong and fast, too."

"Espera." The man who had paid for Mercedes finally spoke up. "Just wait a minute. If you think I want a stupid horse, you're dead wrong. Dead. You understand? I don't care how fast or pretty or whatever it is. I sold *my* horse to get this girl." He squeezed Mercedes arm, and she winced.

John wanted to punch him good right then. Just one strike. It was obvious by the way he held her that whatever he wanted Mercedes for could only mean something bad. Yeah, he could see himself tangling this guy in a one-on-one.

Best to let that go. You're not that man anymore.

And fighting wouldn't do anything but get him dead.

"I wasn't offering her to you." He nodded at Belmonte. "I was suggesting you and I make a little deal. And not for keeps, neither. Just a borrowing kind of deal. Like collateral. Then you and your boy here can settle up whatever way you want."

"Why would I want to do that? How does it benefit me?"

"Well, it's like your boy there said. Might help take some of the heat off from the people in this town." Belmonte's eyes narrowed, and John confirmed his suspicions. "Yeah, that's right. I understood him just fine. But that's not what's important. What really matters is that he was right. Besides, didn't you say that old bird contributes to your supplies? What if that leg's worse than everyone thinks? It'd be a real shame for something to happen to such a nice old gal."

The look in the saloon owner's eyes told John he had won before the man ever said a word.

"You know what, cowboy? I like you." The words were laced with approval. "I will accept your offer of a horse for a woman... *if* the horse is good—"

"Oh, there's nothing to worry about right there. She's about as good as they come – especially in these parts."

"Okay. Deal." Belmonte turned his attention to Mercedes. "Go on and get whatever you need to care for la doña. You will have only three days. And just to make sure you don't try escaping or something, Mocha is going with you."

A look of fright compelled John to learn more. "I'm not so sure about how the old lady would feel with strangers in her home. If you don't mind, who is Mocha?"

"I guess the best way to think of Mocha Orejas is like something of a tailor." Belmonte made a cutting motion with his fingers beside his face, as if removing one of his ears. The implication set off warning bells in John's head, but he remained silent. "Now let's get a look at this horse of yours."

John caught a brief glance of Mercedes as he followed the saloon owner outside. It was but a moment, yet he recognized the look of indifference in her eyes. It was the same one that she wore the first time he had asked her to leave this saloon. It dawned on him then that maybe she hadn't chosen to stay behind because she was afraid to leave. He let out a frustrated sigh. Maybe she hadn't escaped with the others because she *preferred* life as a saloon girl. She didn't really want to leave.

And here I am thinking I'm doing something noble.

John stepped back out into the light of day, the blaze of the sun hitting him strong as he watched the men approach his horse. One unfamiliar hand on her reign, and she reared up. He watched, a sense of helplessness overcoming him, as men flanked her on either side and began pulling.

His blessed horse. A rare chestnut Morgan, as loyal as she was fast. He had used her as a bargaining tool, thinking it would be easy to come back for her in the middle of the night. But as he watched Belmonte and his men drag her to the backside of the saloon, the awful truth hit him. They didn't keep their horses tied up out front. They kept them locked up inside the gate somewhere.

John let out a slow, shaky breath.

What had he done?

Chapter Five

She needed to say *something*.

Mercedes shuffled down the street just a couple of paces behind John. She hadn't been able to take her eyes off him since stepping out of Jericho, and onto the dirt path that brought salvation from the wretched saloon. Was this really happening? After weeks of being cooped up on the property, was she really walking down International Boulevard? And in broad daylight!

To think she owed her freedom to some cowboy she only had the privilege of meeting one time. No wonder she dreamt of him every night! Men like him were rarer than gold pesos. And just as valuable. She would be a fool to let him slip away twice. But from the looks of things, that's exactly what was going to happen. He hadn't said one word – ni una palabrita – since his arrival. Hopefully he wouldn't change his mind about coming back for her. Drastic measures were the last thing she wanted to resort to.

Mercedes turned her attention to the heavy rucksack in her arms, adjusting it so no essentials would fall out. Dried herbs that might help cure the old woman's leg; a few others in case of an emergency. Bringing more would have made

Belmonte suspicious. Even her undergarments and makeup had been left behind. It was worth it to escape, though. That is, if she was indeed escaping.

Her mind back to the cowboy in front of her. Why didn't he speak? Was it because Mocha followed closely behind? Maybe it was all part of his escape plan. He definitely had one of those. Otherwise, how could he return to Jericho? Unless he had spoke the truth, and only needed her services as a medicine woman.

The thought drove her mad. Sí, señor. She definitely needed to say something and find out what he had planned.

"Sure as the sun, this sack is heavy." It was the first thing that popped into her mind, and she figured his response would determine how he viewed her.

She paused to adjust the bag just as he reached back, unceremoniously plucking the it from her arms. His cool indifference spoke volumes. He was in no mood to talk – least of all to someone he had little use for. No. It looked like she'd have to rescue herself, and come up with her own escape plan. She silently fell into step beside him, determined to remain that way, except John immediately stopped short. Mercedes glanced up and spied the formidable Doña Maria standing outside her house, shaking a rug. The woman stopped and glared as the group drew closer. "Um, she doesn't look too happy to see us."

"Just stay here for a moment."

John approached the woman who instantly spat off, switching between rapid-fire Spanish and broken English. How could he bring *basura* to her home? She didn't want some trashy woman touching her leg – which was none of John's business anyway. And el Mocha? She would gather every man in town, including the Villistas, to cut into him if he even thought about crossing her threshold.

"By the love of the Virgin y el Padrecito! Has the whole world gone mad?"

The woman's shrill reminded Mercedes of her mother's reaction when her father had announced his decision to do business with Belmonte. It was the last time she could remember anyone taking a tongue lashing like the one John was receiving. But the patience he displayed! He stood there, listening to her rant before calmly explaining his position on the matter. A few minutes later and they reached an understanding.

Mercedes could stay, provided she slept on a pallet in the main room. Mochas, on the other hand, wasn't stepping a foot indoors. He could do his "guarding" on the front stoop.

John walked back over to the pair.

"Something tells me the two of you already heard the terms and conditions." He addressed Mocha. "Do we need to make different arrangements?"

The man shook his head, stating he preferred the company of a sky full of stars to a screeching banshee that could put la Llorona to shame.

"Alright then." He gave Mercedes a meaningful nod. "Guess you're up."

She stepped forward to greet the woman.

"Buenas, Doña. It's a fine afternoon to—"

"It's not a fine anything when a strange foreigner decides to interfere in your life by bringing trash into your home!" The old woman glowered from the top of her stoop. "Oh, yes. I know *exactly* who and what you are! And by the breath of God, I wouldn't let you come near me – let alone touch me – if my leg didn't hurt so bad."

Mercedes bit down on her tongue to keep her temper in check. She was accustomed to men treating her poorly within the walls of Jericho. However, no woman crossed her path without some kind of retribution.

But John was watching.

She glanced back and got an encouraging nod from him, a small smile gracing his face. The action was enough to give her some small hope that maybe they could still work together, and get away from this town. She turned back to Doña Maria, her words laced with false sweetness.

"Well, then, let us go inside and see what we can do to help you."

Mercedes couldn't believe how well things were going. A few hours prior, Doña Maria wanted to throw her back to the dogs of Jericho. Now they were all conversing, laughing at stories they each shared while the doña served them huevos con frijoles y sopa de arroz. Honestly, she didn't know what tasted better. It was all so good! The eggs, soft and fluffy, were perfectly scrambled. The beans had just the right amount of salt. And the rice? Oh, the red rice! Had she ever tasted anything so lovely? She spooned a little more of it from a Talavera centerplate.

"We never eat like this at the cantina. Well, Señor Belmonte does. The rest of us get by on nopales and tortillas." She winked at their hostess. "But I bet even his meals don't taste *this* good. You're an excellent cocinera, Doña Maria!"

The laughter died a bit at the admission that the girls weren't eating much.

"Ay, hija." The elderly woman shrugged off the compliment. "You did most of the cooking. I just shared my recipes."

"And let's not forget the tortillas!" John scooped a spoonful of his food into one. "These things are great!"

"De veras." Doña Maria agreed with him and helped herself to another one. "Signs of una mujer verdadera."

A real woman.

It was the first time – outside the bedroom leastways – that someone had referred to her as such. Mercedes rolled the thought around her mind. She liked the way it sounded, and beamed up at the elderly patient-turned-hostess.

"Gracias."

"Ay! Y tan bonita?" Doña Maria turned to John, whispering not-so-subtly. "Just look at how pretty she is when she smiles. Really, a man would be foolish to let this one escape."

John choked, his face turning a red that could rival the strands on his head. Violently coughing, he wheezed out "wrong pipe."

Mercedes jumped up to get him some water to drink, but could hardly register her own actions. It was like she was in a dream, moving in slow motion as she tried to wrap her mind around the old woman's brazen remark. Was she really worthy enough to be someone's bride? Would someone like John ever consider her as wifely material? Things seemed to be turning out nicely. At least he was talking to her now. But a wife? Oh, such lofty dreams! She hoped at the very least that they could be companions. Maybe a little more.

She handed him the cup and watched as he quietly drank, the coloring of his face returning back to normal. An awkward silence hung in the air between them.

"Well," Doña Maria pushed herself away from the table. "I guess I should start cleaning up."

"Oh, allow me to help." Mercedes jumped up to assist the woman.

"Nonsense, nena. You haven't even finished your food yet." Despite objections, the woman reached over and spooned out a second helping for her two houseguests. "Never let it be said that anyone has gone hungry while in the home of Doña Maria." She gave a quick nod to the both of them, then picked up the near empty pot of beans and two tortillas before making her way to the outside wash basin.

The old woman's absence filled Mercedes with doubt as an uncomfortable silence settled over the table. She kept her eyes down, focused on her plate of food. Still, every thought revolved around him. Could John want someone like her? Would he claim a secondhand, used up woman? Surely not. He could easily get a younger, prettier girl who didn't have to hide budding wrinkles under gobs of powder. One whose English wasn't so ugly and broken.

Broken English, broken girl.

No, it was too much to wish for. They had yet to even become friends. Besides, it wasn't wise to expect so much from him when it was likely that she was going to be traded right back to Belmonte... for a horse!

Oh, he was still sore about that one for sure. The way he had prayed to his make-believe God to get his horse back? Mercedes had bowed her head with respect, because she was thankful to her hostess for providing such a divine meal. The last thing she expected was a quick "thanks" for the food, sent up with a longer petition about a horse.

Still, a cowboy without his horse was like a meal without the tortillas. The least she could do was apologize. It might even help smooth things over.

"I never had the chance—"

"Well, that there is proof—"

She and John both stopped talking and stared at each other. His face cracked into a wide grin that touched his eyes, and she could see that she had been wrong about the coloring. The green orbs held flecks of blue in them, with a beautiful black ring circling each one. She suddenly realized that she had been staring and cleared her throat.

"Sorry."

"Not at all." John's smile softened, warm and inviting. It gave her a bit of hope. "Ladies first, always."

Mercedes looked down, suddenly shy. "Actually, that's all I was going to say. I just wanted to apologize for everything."

John looked down at his plate for a moment and frowned. Had he grown cold again? Well, she had no one to blame but herself if he did.

"There's no apology needed." His remark surprised her, as did the kindness she saw in his face when he looked back up. She dared to meet his stare. His eyes darkened, raw with emotion. A strange feeling full of promise and desire passed between them, forcing her breath to catch.

She abruptly dropped her gaze. "You were about to say something, too. Yes?"

John cleared his throat.

"Oh, um. Yeah." He opened up the crocheted *sirvilleta* that kept the tortillas warm, and chose one to sop up the thick soup the beans had left behind. "I was just going to say that these tortillas were proof of a good cook."

Mercedes could feel heat creeping up her face. She cooked daily for the men at Jericho. But the idea of complimenting her for it surely never crossed their minds. John's appreciation was a welcomed change, and she would've said so if she didn't think it would ruin the moment.

"The doña even took a couple with her – just to keep up her strength while cleaning."

Mercedes burst out at John's remark.

"What? What did I say?" He sat there, dumbfounded. It only made her laugh harder.

Mercedes wiped her eyes, calming a bit. "Despite the bad leg, I don't think Doña Maria could be considered a weak woman in need of more tortillas."

John chuckled. "She does come off as a force to be reckoned with."

"Yes, I think the tortillas were for the chickens."

"She feeds the chickens tortillas?" John sat back with surprise.

"Claro! It's what everyone here does. Just tear them up into small pieces, and add a little water. They love it! In fact, I remember once when I was little—" Mercedes stopped, a bit dismayed by the sudden recollection of an obscure childhood memory.

"Go on." John prodded her, his voice but a whisper. "When you were little—"

Mercedes stared down at the half-empty plate in front of her. Did she want to share such a precious memory with him? With anyone? She glanced up and searched his face. It held a look of genuine interest. John Durbin, American cowboy who rode into foreign countries to rescue his friends, was genuinely interested in *her*. Not to warm his bed, nor the medicines she could make. At that moment, he just wanted to know more about her.

"When I was little," she began, "One of my chores was to feed the chickens. Well, I had a younger brother. Oh, he was travieso. A naughty little boy, always playing tricks. He would do things like follow me around when I was feeding the chickens. While I was throwing the tortilla pieces, he would pick them up and hide them in his pocket."

John cracked a smile.

"You think that's funny, *eh*?" Mercedes chastised him. "You just wait."

"My mother was always asking me '*Hija, why you no feed the chickens. Apurate!*' and I would tell her that I did, but that Carlitos – that was my brother – had stolen their food. So she would ask him '*You still hungry, hijo?*' and we'd all laugh. Then, of course, she would tell him to give the chickens back their food, or they wouldn't lay anymore eggs, and then he really would be hungry. Pues, that one day he stole the food he went back outside to give it to the chickens. Except this time, I had added a little more water than usual, and the tortillas had turned to mush in his pocket. So there he was, trying to get the mush out of his pockets, and the chickens getting so desperate to eat breakfast, that they just couldn't wait. The next thing you know, Carlitos comes running through the house, screaming como un loco. The chickens are chasing right behind, feathers flying everywhere, all of them singing 'pio, pio' for their food..."

John burst out laughing. Mercedes joined him.

"... took the whole day to clean up the mess they left behind." She slowly calmed. "But for certain, Carlitos learned to never tease the chickens again."

"Sounds like you have a lovely family."

Mercedes stiffened. "Yes, because lovely families always sell their daughters." The words were out before she could stop them, but she wouldn't have taken them back even if she could. Maybe she did have a few nice memories of them. It still didn't change the fact that she had been traded for a bag full of coins. And now here was this handsome cowboy, little more than a stranger, who owed her absolutely nothing. It was only a matter of time before he did the same, and traded her to get his horse back. The idea of being so dispensable filled her with ire, but she refused to lose her composure in front of John.

Standing, she snatched up both their plates and excused herself. "I better help Doña Maria.

She shouldn't be walking around with that leg of hers."

Chapter Six

John's surprise to Mercedes's outburst the night before was nothing compared to the shock he received when he walked out his bedroom the following morning. Doña Maria bustled around the *sala*, an ornate bowl in hand from which she scooped up small pools of water to splash on the floor. Mercedes followed close behind her, sweeping up small clumps of dirt that the water attracted.

"Buenos días, Señor Durmido." Doña Maria continued her ritual. "There's some pan y café en la cocina."

"Thank you." John smiled at the "Sir Sleepy" reference. He fancied the remark something his mother would have said, if he could recall what she had been like. He was about to turn towards the kitchen, the enticing smells of sweet bread and coffee beckoning him, when he caught Mercedes from the corner of his eye.

She and the old woman were engaged in a rather amusing exchange. The woman had grabbed the broom from Mercedes, a jerk of her head suggesting the girl follow John. Mercedes reached out to reclaim the broom only to have the woman turn away, hugging it close to her bent form. She freed one hand and reached behind her, giving Mercedes a decent shove towards the kitchen.

John bit back a laugh and hurried out the room. Mercedes entered, a sweet pout on her freshly washed face. It was the first time he had ever seen her without makeup, and he couldn't help but think how lovely she looked.

And young.

"How old are you?" The words spewed forth, surprising both of them. The question was valid enough, but certainly not a way to begin the day. "My apologies. I meant to say you look nice this morning, and uh, younger without your paints."

Her lips formed a tight line. She didn't respond, busying herself at the stove instead.

John tried to shake off the embarrassment he felt as he watched her move around. The mere presence of this woman made him feel like a boy in grade school again. "Sorry about the way that came out. Although, I was speaking the truth, ma'am. You're quite beautiful."

A half smile touched Mercedes's lips, as if she were trying to keep a straight face. She placed a plate of bread laced with clumps of sugar onto the table, followed by two glazed mugs of black coffee. "My quinceañera was almost ten years ago. So that makes me twenty and five."

John registered the information, but couldn't get past the new Spanish word. "You're what?"

"My *quinceañera*." She offered him the sugar bowl for his coffee, but he waved it away. "It's a celebration that marks when a girl becomes a woman, and she is prepared to become a wife or a monja."

"A what?"

"A nun."

"Oh." John paused to take a sip of his coffee, slowly wrapping his mind around the information. There was a question left unspoken; a black drape of misery hanging over them, threatening to smother anything good that was or could possibly be. But he had to ask. Regardless of the paths they decided to take, it would follow him for the rest of his life if he didn't know.

"Which one were you supposed to be?"

Mercedes stared down into her cup of coffee, hands gripping it so tightly that the white of her knuckles shown. When she finally raised her head, he could see the tears she was fighting back. He reached across the table to gently pry one hand away from the cup and give it an encouraging squeeze. She let out a slow, shaky breath.

"There was a boy in the pueblo." Her eyes glazed over before dropping back down to her mug. "His name was Juan Calendeza. Only two years older than me, but already he had his land. Sickness had fallen on the town the year before and many had died – mostly the very old and little babies, or the ones weak from hunger and hard living. It was a tough year for everyone. But life goes on. It did for the rest of us including Juan who, as the oldest, inherited his family's *hacienda* along with the care of three younger sisters. And that is a lot of work, having to watch over and protect a group of girls while managing the fields. So he visited my father one day, determined to have "the prettiest girl in town." He was eager for us to marry right away, and with seven children of his own to care for, my father was just as happy to marry me off – especially since Juan refused a dowry. Of course, I was excited too. Marriage to Juan meant that I'd only have the girls to care for instead of a pack of brothers. I could take care of my own house and…" Her free hand instinctively fluttered to her stomach. "Any children of my own."

Her eyes grew dreamy, as if trying to recapture a past that held no place for her, but refused to set her free. John gave her hand another soft squeeze, but she remained transfixed to that place even after she continued.

"My mother prepared me for misa that morning." Her eyes closed. "I had never worn such a beautiful dress before – so different from the bright colors worn at fiestas like el Día de La Santa Cruz or Día de Los Muertos. This one was white with laced sleeves, soft and fluffy like clouds." A smile momentarily graced her, a quiet hum escaping her. "I even had boots to match."

Mercedes opened her eyes again, the smile fading as her face hardened. "So I went to church for the misa – to show that I was still an honest woman before man and God. No one in Juan's family attended, and I was a little surprised at that. See, the fiesta for my quinceañera was to be held at the Calendeza estate, because my family was quite poor, and our home much too tiny for a celebration. So we walked from the church to Juan's home. All of us. Well, I sat on a mule to not ruin the hem of my dress, but the rest of the family and friends walked."

Mercedes pulled her hand away from John, the action leaving him suddenly cold. She lifted the coffee and took a sip, a look of disgust painting her face as she swallowed.

"They were dead." She placed the cup back down, and tightly folded her hands. "All of them. From little Máte to Juan, they had all been slaughtered like animals and worse. The girls had been playing in the garden with their dolls, feeding them from tiny teacups. It looked like Juan tried to protect them from the soldiers, or at least save their innocence. But what is one rifle against a dozen? They claimed the terreno as government land. And when the last soldier was finally finished satisfying himself, we were allowed to claim the bodies."

"My mother and I helped put their dresses back on while the men dug the graves." Mercedes's voice grew soft. "Then I gave them their dollies, so they wouldn't be all alone."

Silence settled over them like a thick blanket. John swallowed past the lump in his throat, disgust settling in the pit of his stomach.

He wanted to announce the difference between the soldiers from his own country, but the record numbers of those that visited the Jericho saloon kept his mouth shut. There might not have been a land war involved, but their other theft couldn't be denied.

He pushed the thought away. "Is that when you ended up with Belmonte?"

Mercedes nodded. "Sí. The soldiers were still there when he passed through town the following week. El Señor Belmonte was a new face at Sunday mass, and seemed like a real caballero. A gentleman who knew when to kneel; when to pray. He displayed righteous anger when he heard about the Calendeza family, acting as a father would when he heard how the girls were disgraced. It didn't take long for him to convince my father to sell me, all under the pretense of marrying me off to a husband with a good home. Both my parents agreed that it was a better choice than risking the chance of some soldier claiming me. He even paid them. 'The loss of a daughter,' he called it."

"I'm sorry for what happened." John reached back out, attempting to take hold of her hand again. However, Mercedes quickly placed it in her lap instead.

"Thank you, but I don't need your pity. It happened long ago. In fact, so long ago that I didn't even remember that day until you asked about it."

"Again, my apologies." It seemed the only thing he could say this morning. Sorry for this, sorry for that. He wanted to give himself a good, swift kick. Didn't he have anything better to offer? Something more than wasteful words that couldn't change the past? With the way she was talking, it didn't seem like she much cared for Belmonte or working in his saloon. Perhaps she would leave with him this time.

Maybe if he stopped beating around the bush, and asked her how —

"Día de La Madre!" Doña Maria stood in the entranceway, a fist firmly planted on each hip. "I send you two in here for breakfast, and no one even looks at the pan. What were you both doing? Talking to the santos?"

"Ay, Doña. Don't get so upset." Mercedes picked up the bread plate and offered it to John. "We were just about to eat. Right, John?"

"Oh, um. Right, right." John grabbed a roll from the plate and took a bite. "Mmmm."

Doña Maria waved off the explanation. "Too late. La Lupita is here now."

"La Lupita?" Mercedes stood, dropping the bread back onto the plate. "La Fea!"

John took another bite of his roll, his mouth partially full. "Interesting that Belmonte let your friend out."

Mercedes only shrugged. "It's nothing new. La Fea has a rather interesting arrangement with Belmonte. Although, I couldn't say what it is.

She's allowed a lot more liberties than the rest of the girls, though."

John turned to Doña Maria. "Well, why did she come? Is there something urgent?"

"Sabe?" The woman shrugged. "Something about your wild horse."

John jumped up from the table, nearly knocking the chair over as he bolted from the room. The two women slow to follow.

"You're sure he said that?" John had already wrung out an explanation from the messenger when the women walked in. He looked as excited as a *lobo* that just caught the scent of his next meal.

"Sí, señor." La Fea backed away. "El Señor Belmonte will put her down if you don't come right away."

John dashed out the door, one hand holding down his hat. The other clutched the pistol at his waist.

Chapter Seven

The wooden pestle felt heavy in Mercedes's hand from the continual grounding. The stone mortar had been worn smooth from years of use, offering less than desired results. Plus, she had to keep stopping as Doña Maria flitted behind her from one side to the other, questioning Mercedes's every movement. The constant stop-and-go made the task take twice as long as expected.

"And that one?" The woman pointed to a small bag on the table. "What does that one do?"

Mercedes tried to disguise her annoyance, reminding herself that the woman's hospitality was far better than the treatment she received at Jericho.

Even if had spent more than half the day helping the woman complete chores. Cooking, cleaning, feeding the chickens, and helping out in the garden. It was hard work, but it gave her something to do other than think about John.

John.

What could possibly be taking so long? What if Belmonte had—

"Answer me, hija, or I'm not drinking it! Could be the devil's brew for all I know."

Mercedes's attention snapped back to the woman. She reached into her leather pouch for a few leaves of the belladonna she carried. "It will help you sleep."

"De veras? How come?" The woman crossed her arms, raising one skeptical brow as she eyed her houseguest. "Is that even safe?"

Mercedes sighed, a vague hint of disbelief lacing her words. "Ay, Doña. You really don't know anything at all about making medicines? A woman your age? I'm not so sure I believe that."

"It's true, mi'ja!"

"How is possible that someone who can make such delicious, flavorful food with so many different spices doesn't know anything at all about the plants I carry? You're telling me that you can't make tea to relieve a headache, or paste to lower a child's fever?"

"Well, I've never had children. So I've never had to cure a fever for one. And headaches? I'm a Reyes, nena." She pounded her chest for emphasis. "I just tough those out when they come. As for the spices, well, I trade for those. Then I just add what I think tastes good."

The woman found a chair and sat, rubbing her bad leg. It was looking much better, the swelling having gone down significantly. However, it was obvious that the morning's cleaning spree had aggravated it. Mercedes made a mental note to add some *manzanilla* to the mixture.

"I guess I just assumed that you would have had a whole pack of bebitos, all grown up with children of their own by now."

"Ay, que no." La Doña waved the idea off. "Not saying that I didn't want them, of course. I guess, Dios just didn't see fit for me to have a family."

There He was again.

God.

A snort of disgust slipped from Mercedes's tight-lipped grimace. The woman quirked a wrinkled brow. "What was that, nena?"

Mercedes slammed down the pestle and turned on the woman, a hand placed firmly on one hip. "Why do people do that? Why do they credit everything to some make-believe man in the sky?" She turned back to the table and picked up the mortar, dumping the contents into one of the clay *ollas*. "Are there so few *good* men left on Earth that we've got to go searching the Heavens for them?"

"You would know better than me, chiquita. The guard may be stationed at my door, but I'm not the one he's watching."

Mercedes quietly placed the mortar back onto the table, then shuffled towards the *sala*, stopping just outside the entryway between the two rooms. She leaned against its frame. From her spot she could spy the front door, open to allow a rare breeze into the adobe home – the only redemption for such a hot summer day. However,

Mocha's silhouette loomed in the light, threatening to block that bit of happiness.

Mercedes's voice dropped to a tremulous whisper. "If there is a God, then el diablo is real, too. And that one right there will be his right-hand man." She cocked her head, a knowing nod in the woman's direction. "Proof there's no good ones left!"

"I don't know if I'd say all that, girl. What about your John?"

The sound of his name produced a longing for something Mercedes hadn't dared to dream of since she was a young woman – the one who had prepared to become the mistress of a ranch many years ago. Could she still have something like that? Was it even possible? She had begun to open up to him yesterday, share a bit of who she was, but he had yet to do the same.

She ran her hands down the front of her skirt.

No. It could never be. He could probably accept her past, and some of the secrets that had accumulated over the years. But not the one she carried now.

"I don't know what you're talking about." She shrugged off the thought of some "happily ever after."

"No, no, amor. You can't lie to me. I've seen the way you look at him, and the way he looks at you, too. Why do you think I insisted that you sleep in the great room… on the floor?" Doña Maria let out an exasperated sigh. "You think I'm so mean as to make a medicine woman sleep on the floor?"

Laughter bubbled out before Mercedes could stop it. "People call me a lot of things, Doña, but 'medicine woman' has never been one of them!"

"Listen to the way you talk!" The woman shook a reprimanding finger at her. "You know what your problem is? You don't know your worth!"

"Yes I do." Mercedes grew serious, the fleeting moment of mirth abruptly dying. "Twenty pesos for twenty minutes; fifty for an hour. And if you're willing to part with two hundred coins, then you can have me all night."

Doña Maria stared at her for a moment, as if weighing the words and determining their value. She finally forced herself out of the chair and walked away from the table, past Mercedes and into the *sala*.

Well, I guess that did it. Now she's going to throw you out.

Mercedes knew her time had come to an end, and refused to turn around to watch La Doña in action. She would face this moment with as much dignity as possible, and wait for the old woman to return with El Mocha. Then she would finally be able to give up the silly notion about marrying some redhead cowboy.

The sound of the woman shuffling behind her forced her upright, her back rigid with anger. She spun around, ready to face the devil himself.

"Ten." Doña Maria stood in front of her, a Bible in one outstretched hand. "You'll have to read for me. My eyes are too old."

Mercedes clucked her tongue at the woman. "Ay, nada nada con tú biblia."

She waved the book off, wanting nothing to do with it.

"Oye, chiquita. You can do whatever you want when you're out in the streets or in la cantina, or wherever else you go. But when you're in my house, you'll do as I say. Entiendes?"

Mercedes's jaw dropped. She snapped her mouth closed again, taking the Bible with only slight hesitation. "You sure you've never been a madre? You sure talk like one!"

"Of course I do! I was the oldest of eleven children. Eleven! So I did plenty of mothering."

"Eleven children, and not a single one to help you when you injured your leg?" Mercedes shook her head with disbelief, but the woman forged on.

"Well, that's because there's only two of us left in this pueblo. Several have moved away, married with families and responsibilities. Two ran off to make money in el Norte. They say some place in the east. And four others serve el Padrecito." She let out a sigh, finally running out of steam, and crossed herself. "God rest their souls."

A remembrance from child rose up in her, a tingling on her fingertips to copy the woman's gesture. She tamped it down, flipping open the cover of the Bible instead.

"It's in English!"

"Yes." Doña Maria sat in her seat again, shifting to find a comfortable position. "That's how I learned to speak and read the language. The writing is not so good still."

"That's wonderful." Mercedes pulled out a chair for herself. She flipped open the book, the words a deluge of foreign symbols that held no meaning for her. She studied them a moment longer, then raised her gaze with confusion. "I know how to say just about anything, but I'm not very good with the paper part. I guess the words are just easier to hear."

The woman chuckled. "Some good we do each other. I, who cannot see, and you who cannot read."

"Then I guess that's the end of that." Mercedes snapped the cover shut, thankful to not have to struggle over the strange words.

"Not so fast!" Doña Maria motioned for her to open the book again. "We can at least try to find the scripture I had in mind. Flip towards the back of the book for Luke."

She made the shape of an "L" with her hand.

The two women thumbed through versus until the warmth of crimson light bathed the heavens. They took turns trying to find the right scripture, sounding out the letters once they did.

"Qué bueno!" La Doña nodded with approval. "You're doing very well – especially considering that even this English is very old now."

"It doesn't look like anything I've seen before."

"And you probably never will outside this copy, or the one el Padre reads from."

"How did you even get it?"

"A friend gave it to me long ago – una monja. Except she never did become a nun. She was going to, though. But then she passed away." Doña Maria cleared her throat and waved the thought away. "Well, it was many years ago. Then el Padre Emmanuel came for a visit. That's when I got it."

Mercedes tenderly ran her fingers along the Bible. "So much sadness seems to be attached to this book. Both the people who live in it, and the ones who read it, suffer too much."

"Ah, yes. But that isn't God's fault. That comes from the Enemy." The woman bobbed her head. "Just remember what it says in the scripture we just read. Go on. Read it again."

Mercedes squinted at the letters, silently reading it once before speaking. "Are not five sparrows sold for two farthings, and not one of them is forgotten before God? But even the very hairs of your head are all numbered: Fear not therefore—"

" —ye are of more value than many sparrows."

The baritone sound of a familiar voice surprised her.

"John!" She dropped the book onto the table, jumping up to greet him. Impulse propelled her forward, her arms wrapping around him in a warm embrace. The feel of strong muscles beneath a thin cotton shirt felt welcoming.

Not to mention the return embrace.

She could have continued standing there forever except the doña chose that moment to excuse herself from the room, a loud "eh hem" signaling her exit.

Suddenly reminded of where and what she was, Mercedes snapped back. Her hands flew up to cover her face, shame washing over. She berated herself for acting like a wanton saloon girl. Slowly lifting her head, she hardly dared to look John in the face. "I'm so sorry. I don't know what came over me."

She waited for him to go cold on her. Instead, his eyes grew soft with obvious desire. He reached out, a thumb gently trailing down the side of her cheek. "No need to apologize, darlin.' I ain't complaining none. In fact, if I may be so bold, I kinda' liked it."

Heat rose to her face. Was the balmy day to blame, or the burn of his touch? She quickly looked away, out the kitchen window. The warmth of crimson light that bathed the heavens couldn't compare to the glow Mercedes felt within.

"Um… it's kind of late para la comida, but I can light a fire if you'd like to cenar." She clenched the front of her skirt with nervousness, then ran her hands down her belly, smoothing the fabric again.

John's expression suggested that he hungered for something more than food, but he only nodded. "That'll be just fine."

She hurried out the back door of the kitchen to the brick *fogón* a few paces away from the house. The *olla* was still half full; the beans warm. A bright red still burned from the smoldering embers below. She lifted two small logs from beside the outdoor oven and tossed them in. A few stokes with a metal rod and they were soon ablaze.

"Need any help?"

Mercedes jumped again, a nervous laugh escaping her. "You're quieter than the coyote who stole the chicken!"

John laughed a rich chuckle that made her smile. "It's something that comes in handy from time to time."

Mercedes thought back to when they first met. "Like when we helped Catalina escape?"

The air grew still between them, the silence drawing out.

"Yeah. Something like that." Hands in his pocket, he looked down at a patch of browning grass. "You know I always wondered about you staying behind. Why was that?"

She turned away from him, busying herself at the stove by giving the pot a stir. "I don't know. I guess it just didn't seem right. I mean, I hardly knew Catalina let alone you. Perhaps I would have been trading one nightmare for another."

"And now?" John placed a hand on her shoulder. Slowly turning her around, his deep green eyes burrowed into her soul. "Would you want to go with me, or still live in that... place?"

She studied him for a moment, thinking about the scripture she read earlier – about God caring for her more than the sparrows. Was this what He meant? Was this the way He'd take care of her?

No.

She squeezed her eyes shut and pushed the thought from her head. She wasn't about to buy into that fairytale only to wake up and find it was all a lie. There was no God. She was on her own in this. Well, sort of. She protectively wrapped her arms around herself. She should tell him what had happened? How would he react if he knew she'd been raped? Not that it had been the first time, but the last few weeks...

"So, what say you?" John wiggled a bushy auburn brow. He gave her a mischievous grin. "You'll never have to set foot this side of the border again. Plenty of chickens in North Carolina to chase us around all we want."

Mercedes couldn't help but smile. "I do want to go with you... but I —"

"That's the ticket!" John took his hat off and victoriously slapped it against his leg. "We'll have to wait a few days until Abby's leg is a bit better.

"Abby's leg?"

"Yeah, that's why I was down there so long. One of them boys got it in his head to try to mount her. Who'd do a fool thing like that, I'll never know." He chuckled. "But she sure did get him good. Bucked him clear across the corral."

His smile faded and he became serious again. "Of course, she did hurt herself pretty bad coming down."

Mercedes let out a gasp. She knew that a horse injury could mean death for the poor animal if not treated properly. "Is she going to be okay?"

"She will be if you're willing to help."

"What do you mean?"

Hesitating, John ran a hand through his hair. "I kind of made a deal with Belmonte."

"Uh. What kind of deal?"

"Well, um. Basically, that you stay here – mixing up some stuff I can use to heal Abby, and helping out Doña Maria until my horse pulls through."

"And if the injury doesn't heal? If you have to put her down?"

John squeezed the hat in his hand, glancing out into the red evening sky. Mariachi music from a neighboring house echoed into the descending night. He let out a slow breath, then finally looked back at her.

"If she goes down, then I keep you."

Chapter Eight

Three days. Three stinkin' days.

That's how long had passed and Mercedes still hadn't spoken more than a handful of words to him.

John chewed on a piece of juniper as he rubbed the horse's leg with the salve Mercedes had made. The ointment had been waiting for him the morning after their... talk. Fixing to head down to the saloon to check on Abby, he found it on the kitchen table. A little note had accompanied it.

"For Abby. Hope it helps."

That's what their communication consisted of now. Morning notes and curt words at mealtimes of please and thank you – most of which was probably being directed at Doña Maria anyways. The old woman tried her hardest to fill the silence. John learned more about Mexican history than he ever thought he even wanted to. Not that he was complaining.

Sure would've been nice to learn more about Mercedes, though.

But could he blame her? He had divulged so little information about himself – not that his life had been all that interesting anyway. It's not like he had done anything truly notable. Although he was fairly certain the real problem was with what he *had* done.

He had treated Mercedes no different (well, okay, maybe a little different) from the men at the saloon. It wasn't like he was taking advantage of her. At least, not in the physical sense. Her help really was needed for Abigail, though. For all he knew, she had taken it the wrong way. And agreeing to trade her against a dead horse? Well, it wasn't exactly the most romantic idea.

Romantic?

John paused. Where had that idea come from? He had returned to Mexico in hopes of doing the right thing. Save the girl... not fall for her!

"Aw, who am I foolin,' Abby?" John started wrapping the horse's leg again. He stood and ran a hand down it's sleek hair. "I knew there was something going on the first time I saw her. Crazy, isn't it?"

The horse snorted.

"All right." John adjusted his hat. "Don't go rubbing it in now. And don't go getting into any more trouble! I'll be checking on you in the morning to make sure of that."

He gave the horse one last pat, then made his way out of the stall, back down the crumbling adobe corridor towards the enclosed garden. He paused at the end of wall, voices drifting his way.

"Come on, honey. You want the clients to be happy, right?"

"Aw, Billy." A younger voice spoke. "Leave that one alone."

"Shut up, Tom!"

John heard the muffled sound of a feminine voice. He carefully peered around the corner.

What do those boys think they're doing?

There was no mistaken the two American soldiers who had questioned John when he was stateside. Still a couple of wet-behind-the-ear young guns, except this time they were looking for trouble. They stood in the opposite corner, a young woman pinned between the corner wall and the larger of the two.

"I'm serious, Billy!" The scrawnier comrade squeaked. "That Belmonte guy said this one isn't available."

"Must mean she's extra special." His friend laughed. "Old coot's keeping her for himself!"

The girl struggled against the man's weight, another muffled cry escaping.

"Stop lying to yourself, and let's go before something happens! You don't want none of that anyway. Look at how dirty she is. Might get something nasty."

"Nah. She just needs a little spit and shine. Ain't that right, honey?"

The girl violently jerked, struggling as the man's hand traveled the length of her body, finding every opportunity to invade her privacy.

That's the last straw.

John stepped out from the shadows and casually leaned against the wall. ""Hey, partner.

Ask me, your lady friend there doesn't seem too interested in your offer."

Startled, both boys straightened up to face John, the first with a slight wobble in his movement.

John let out a sigh. He had enough problems of his own right now. The last thing he wanted to do was fight some kid who obviously didn't know how to handle his drink. At the same time, he couldn't just let one of Mercedes's friends be abused – especially when he was standing right there. He'd never forgive himself.

"How 'bouts you go and sleep off some of that drink, son?" John slowly fingered the butt of his pistol, the old habit of a gunslinger hardly masking the words of a former sheriff.

"Aw, heck, Billy." The younger, backed away from his friend. "Come on. Let's go! Don't you remember that man crossing last week? That there's the law."

Billy spat, defiance oozing in every movement. "Yeah? Well, he ain't got no say on this side of the line. Ain't that right, old man?"

Old? Why that no good, sorry excuse for a —

If John couldn't get by on respect, then intimidation would have to do.

"Listen to your friend, son. I'd hate to have to bury ya' on such a fine day."

The young man balked. "You talking to *me*? Why, you've done lost your mind." He turned to his comrade, grabbing him by the collar and pulling him forward. "C'mon! Let's get him!"

His friend shook him off. "This ain't what I signed on for. You said we was gonna' get some drinks. Shoo! I got me a girl back home. You want this dirty one so bad, then you go and get him!"

The young soldier turned and headed back into the saloon, leaving his comrade to stare after him.

"It's Billy, right?" John didn't wait for a response. "Well, you've got yourself a good friend there, Billy boy. I suggest you do the same as him. Now head on back to find something more to your liking."

"Hey, mister. Who do you think you are?" The soldier produced a low, feral growl. He lunged forward, one raised fist ready to strike.

Lightning-quick, John drew his gun. The cold steel planted into the young man's chest.

"Don't make me do something we'll both regret."

The promise of death laced each word, but it was no deterrent for the wayward soldier. His hand snapped to his waist, fingers wrapping around the pistol hanging there. He hardly got the gun out of the holster. John flipped his own piece around, holding it by the barrel. He brought it down on the side of Billy's head. It created a muted *clunk*. The soldier slipped to his knees, falling forward into a wasted heap.

Using the toe of one boot, John gave the fella a solid push. He rolled over with a lazy flop. Once the steady rhythm of his chest rising and falling indicated he was fine, John turned to the girl.

"Are you okay?" He reached a hand out for the saloon worker, trying to ignore her filthy clothes and ragged hair. "Hey, I know you. You're that girl who delivered the message about my Abigail. What'd they call you? Fea or something? Not that I think the name's fitting or nothing."

Hand still outstretched, he hoped the chatter would ease her out of her obvious fright. It proved successful when she finally latched onto him, her shaking body easing around the fallen soldier before her.

"They're all the same," she whispered, slipping her arm into the crook of his.

John followed her gaze to her attacker. "No, they really aren't." He patted her hand with assurance. "We have some amazing men overseas, doing all sorts of heroics to save the lives of people they've never even met – people who aren't even their countrymen."

"That's not what I meant." Fea shook her head. A sound of disgust slipped from her lips. She didn't elaborate further, but John knew what she was referring to.

Men.

He felt bad for her, but could offer little in the way of comfort. "Well, maybe you'll change your mind one day. That is, find someone who'll change your mind for you."

"You mean, someone like you?"

John shifted, unease settling into his spirit. Had he given this young lady the wrong idea? That was the last thing he had intended. But with their arms latched together as they were…

"Um… Well." He could feel sweat collect around the rim of his hat. Swiping it off his head, he ran a the back of one arm across his forehead, then snapped the hat back on. "You could probably find someone even better. Maybe even one of those soldier boys I was telling you about."

"Ach." Fea scrunched up her nose at him. "I wouldn't take to one of those boys even if they paid me a year's worth of wages!"

"Well, never say never. You might just change your mind one day." John gave her a slight tug towards the saloon. He didn't like the idea of delivering any woman to a place like Jericho – especially one that produced clientele like the one he just knocked out. But the chance of Fea forming some sort of attachment to him? Well, that was just out of the question.

"No. I just finished thinking about it, and I will never change my mind." Fea dropped John's arm when he reached for the door. "I will *never* care for a soldier. But someone like you? Yes, that would do just fine."

John swallowed. He released the door handle and turned to the woman he had just rescued.

"Listen. I'm flattered. Really, I am. But I'm sorry if I gave you the impression about being interested in something." John flustered. "I mean, not that someone couldn't be interested in somethin' witcha. I'm sure they could if it was the right someone.

Fea let out a laugh. "Don't worry. I said someone *like* you. I didn't say I wanted the original."

John felt the pent up air slowly leave his chest. *That was a relief!*

"Besides," Fea held up both fists as though preparing to fight, "Mercedes would send me back two full moons if she thought I was batting my eyes at you."

She made her way through the threshold, and he followed after her.

"So you say."

"Has she removed her *pañuello* yet?

"Her what?"

Fea circled a finger above her head. "You know. The cloth she has wrapped around her hair."

"Oh, that?" John paused for a minute. "Come to think on it... No. Why?"

"Uh huh. Just as I thought."

John tried to figure what she meant as they walked down the corridor leading back into the saloon's main room. As if the two men outside hadn't been enough to remind John why he disliked the place, the rowdy display inside certainly did. A couple of men stood in the center of the room, circling one another. He immediately recognized one of them as the younger soldier who had been outside.

"I tell ya, I ain't done nothing!"

The other man – one of Belmonte's henchmen – released an obnoxious laugh before giving the boy a strong shove. He staggered into a table full of patrons, a couple of whom had a trollop on their laps.

The boy stood back up, and one of the men at the table planted a boot in his backside.

"Ándale!"

The boy flew forward again, and landed right into the henchman's fist. He slumped down to the ground, a hand to his jaw.

The crowd whooped, several of them waving money in the air.

Lord, is there anything good at all about this place?

A blur raced past John, and he realized it was the soldier, Billy, that he himself had coldcocked out back. The man had awoken with an obvious urge for vengeance; the idea of a comrade in trouble unacceptable. He plowed into Belmonte's guard like a train. Then he began to pummel him.

An immediate uproar sounded from the crowd, boos and hisses about an unfair fight. One of the betting men raced forward, grabbing Billy by the arms. The man he had slugged stood back up and swung just as another hothead dove into the center of the ring. He threw out the kind of wild punches that only a drunk dog would, not really caring who he struck as long as he got someone. His interference elicited another cry from the crowd and several more men hustled in to fight.

"Come on!" John yanked Fea by the arm, away from the bar brawl. "This is bound to get uglier than a rattlesnake."

They made a beeline for the front door, stopping only long enough to dodge a man tumbling past them. A young gun came right behind.

With a fist held high, ready to wallop the first face it met, the assailant came flying at John. He sidestepped it and the man continued forward. John gave him a swift kick.

"Just helping you along, Son!"

They reached the front door and he pushed Fea out into the light of day.

"Whew! Is it always that bad in there?"

"Sometimes worse."

"No fooling?" John moved down the wooden boardwalk, away from the saloon. Fea followed. "How come you girls don't leave?"

Fea gave him an incredulous look. "How can you ask that? You're not blind. You just saw all the men in that place. What do you think? They're just gonna' let all the girls up and ride off with any gringo that stumbles into Jericho?"

John paused at the end of the walk, his hands at his waist. He scanned the town before him, the adobe homes with their makeshift market lining the streets. The colorful tents made it seem like a world away from what he just walked out of. Why didn't the townsfolk do something? Why didn't they elect a sheriff or something?

"Naw. I guess you're right. Most of those girls can't just up and walk off." He turned back and gave her a once over. "But you could. Mercedes, too. From what I've seen and heard, the two of you were allowed to pretty much roam these parts. Why didn't you gals leave then?"

Fea cracked a smile. "I don't think you really care as to why *I* didn't leave. You want to know why Mercedes didn't go with you."

John stared for a moment, measuring her words. Was she right? Was that the thing itching him the most?

"Yeah, I guess that's got something to do with it. I mean, you give a gal a chance at redemption and she chooses to stay in a cathouse like this... then she blows hot and cold when you return? Well, let's just say it sets a man to thinking something's amiss upstairs." John tapped the side of his head.

Fea rolled her eyes. "Well, what did you think it was going to be? Flowery words and kisses for buying her a few days away from Jericho? No, señor. You need to *do* something. Something that will get her away from here for good, and in a place so far that no one will even want to go looking for her."

"I know, and I've been working on a plan for that. Kind of hard with the hand I've been dealt, though. A lame horse holed up in the innards of Jericho, and an ear-cutting lunatic guarding Mercedes night and day, ain't exactly what I call a winning combination."

John stormed towards the market. Fea followed a few paces behind.

"Then start smaller. Look for another angle." They came upon a puesto full of colorful cloths. She slowed down and ran one hand over a pretty blue revolso. She picked it up. Suddenly turning to him, she smiled. "Isn't this so much nicer than the red sash the girls at Jericho wear?"

John took the shawl and studied it for a moment.

"It sure will be."

Chapter Nine

"The least you can do is keep out of my way. You know?" Mercedes stood on the front stoop, furiously sweeping around Mocha who only leaned back in his chair. He stretched his feet out a little further.

"Well, I'd be out of your way if I was inside." He gave her a crooked smile. "How about inviting me in? Show me what you're cooking today."

Mercedes made a sound of disgust. "I'd rather dine with the devil."

"Who's to say you wouldn't be?"

She swept up a cloud of dust over his boots. "There. That's what I'm serving for dinner."

Mocha snorted. "You're lucky I was told to only watch you." He angled his head and gave her a once over. "Not that watching hasn't had its benefits."

Mercedes ignored the taunt and turned to go back inside, but paused when she saw a figure in the distance.

John!

It had to be him. He had been gone the better part of the day, and she missed having him around – even if most of it had been spent in silence. There was just something about his presence.

She squinted her eyes as he walked closer, making his way down the street, one arm full of colorful cloths and the other...

"Looks like you've been replaced, amor."

She didn't reply, instead focusing on the two coming down the street. Why were they carrying bundles? More importantly, why were they latched arm-in-arm? Fea knew how she felt about John. She wouldn't go after him.

Would she?

A feeling of dread welled up inside. Maybe it had been wrong to punish John so. Three days of refusing to say no more than the necessary pleasantries would drive anyone away. Besides, had his arrangement really been *that* bad? She had reasoned that he was using her like a sack of feed in some sick, twisted barter. But that wasn't really true. She could see that now. He was just trying to make the best of a bad situation.

And she had felt a kindred spirit in John. His eyes soft with understanding as she shared her story. The feel of his arms wrapped around her in response to her eager embrace. He wanted her, too. She had felt it.

So why was he walking with Fea?

She could feel her temperature rise, and she knew it wasn't just from the summer heat. Anger was boiling up inside her. Was he trying to teach her a lesson for not speaking to him? Or was he really interested in her friend?

Who knew what had transpired during the past three days at Jericho?

A snort from Mocha startled her. The man grinned like he had just eaten the last tortilla. Was Mocha planting seeds of doubt in her mind?

One of those scriptures Doña Maria was always having her read suddenly popped into her mind. Something in the Bible book called Mark about a mountain being thrown into the sea. She couldn't remember exactly what had been said, but she remembered what it was about.

"Aléjate de mí, Satanás!" Mercedes glared at a surprised Mocha who, for the first time she could ever recall, made no reply.

She glanced at John once more, and caught his eye. He smiled up at her, raised his hand, and then hesitated before giving her a brief wave. Mercedes responded with a small nod, then looked over to Fea. She squinted at the girl real hard.

Would she get the message that Mercedes questioned her motives?

Fea's eyes widened a little, a knowing smirk tugging at the corner of her mouth. She gave her head a little shake, as if answering the silent questions that burned in her friend's mind. Mercedes glanced away. She no longer felt as though she was about to burn up from within, but a tiny trace of mistrust still lingered in her mind. She turned on her heel and reentered the house.

Once inside, she set off for the kitchen, placing the broom against the corner wall as she passed though the threshold. Her eyes landed on the bag of herbs left on the table from when she made Doña Maria's daily dosage.

Maybe I should...

She snatched up the satchel.

Manzanilla would help calm her nerves, but there was still that other pressing matter. She was counting the days, and there were only a few more left. Nearly one whole month since the first attack at the saloon, and her body showed no signs of the usual monthly pains.

It was time to face facts.

She was with child.

She slowly unwound the string around the bag. There had never been a need for the Poleo before. At least, not for herself. She withdrew a small, dried plant with lavender flowers and studied it. The bit of pennyroyal came from a foreign merchant passing through to el Norte as part of payment for services rendered. He taught her how to use it, and she had made good use of the plant, brewing it for other women at Jericho for a little side money. Not enough to get away, but enough to position herself as head lady of the house – a useful commodity for Belmonte when complications arose from the women's romantic engagements.

She rubbed one bud between her fingers. Too much of the tincture would kill a person. Too little left the boss a pregnant woman who couldn't do her job well. No wonder he wouldn't let her go.

She was the only one who knew the correct amount to brew.

The urge to make the special tea overcame her.

"Qué haces, hija?"

Startled, Mercedes dropped the bag on the table and turned. Her fingers closed around the herb, hiding it in the palm of her hand.

"Doña Maria." She gave the old lady a false smile. "What are you doing out of bed?"

"I couldn't sleep." The woman leaned against the doorframe, arms crossed in front of her chest. She raised a single brow. "And you, girl? You haven't answered my question. What are you doing?"

Mercedes looked away at the doña's accusing eyes. "Nothing really," she said with a shrug.

"Oh, no?" Eyes on Mercedes's clenched fist, the vieja lifted her chin a little. "What do you have there?"

Mercedes glanced down at her hand. She slowly opened it. "This? Oh, it's nothing. Just one of the herbs I sometimes use. I was thinking of making tea, but—"

"Good idea." Doña Maria shuffled over to a table and pulled out a chair. "I could use a tea."

"Oh, no, señora. You won't like the way this one tastes. Let me make you another." Her hand dove into the bag to find another herb instead when the woman wrapped one wrinkled hand around hers.

"Perhaps I don't know about all the plants you keep in that tiny bag of yours, but I do know about that one." She gave Mercedes's hand a good squeeze. "Don't kill your baby."

Mercedes felt the blood drain from her face.

"What makes you think I'm having one?"

"Ay, nena." The doña wagged a finger at her. "I'm old – not stupid."

"Well, it's not for certain yet." Her voice barely a whisper, she slowly sunk into the chair across from Doña Maria. "There's a good possibility that you're right, though. I was attacked almost a month ago. So if nothing happens within the next few days, then I guess I'll know for sure."

She studied the woman with curiosity. "How did you know anyway?"

"Ay, hija. Did you think you're the only one with a past? I have one, too, you know. It's a little different from the one you had. Maybe not as cruel, but there is still plenty of pain in it. That is what makes us women, though. How we handle the pain. That is what makes a man, too. How *they* handle problems. Take your John for instance."

"*My* John?"

The old woman made a guttural sound. She waved away the girl's response. "I won't get into the whole enchilada of you two tiptoeing around the facts. He didn't return to Mexico for the drinks. You know?"

Mercedes nervously bit her bottom lip. "I suppose that's true. Although, I still don't know if I'd go so far as to say he's mine."

"You're right, hija. He most certainly won't be if you don't show a little more calor." The doña shook a finger at her. "Mind you, I'm not saying you should do *any* of those things Belmonte forced you into at the saloon. But the least you could do is act appreciative that he bought you a few days of freedom. Sabe? Things go right, and he might just sweep you off your feet and away from here."

Leave Jericho? That's what Mercedes had wanted ever since the day she watched Catalina ride off into the sunset with her cowboy, John trailing behind them. She remembered the way he asked her to ride with him.

Mercedes felt a surge of hope.

"Do you really think that's possible?"

"Sí, hija. He's a real caballero. The kind that rides in and saves the day. Why, it's already going through town he did just that not even an hour ago."

"He did just… Wait a minute." Mercedes cocked a brow at the woman. "How would you know any of his dealings at all? I thought you were asleep."

"I was!" The woman looked sheepish. "Earlier today."

Mercedes let out a sigh of exasperation. "Doña! You know you need to rest if you want your leg to completely heal."

"Ay, don't worry about my leg. Worry about what happened at Jericho today!"

Mercedes gasped. She hoped whatever it was didn't have anything to do with John. "What happened at the saloon?"

"Well…" Doña Maria shared the little bit she knew from what she saw from a market stand. "I returned and slipped through the back while you were out front, arguing with that perro, Mocha."

Mercedes sat, dumbstruck. The man didn't cease to amaze her. If he wasn't trying to rescue his friends from Jericho, then he was out trying to save one of hers.

"He really is a good man."

"Sí, hija." The woman nodded emphatically. She grabbed up the girl's hand again. "Aren't you tired of getting nothing but toads all the time? Wouldn't it be nice to have a prince instead?"

Mercedes let out a dry laugh. All her determination to never believe in fairytales, and she meets a man who belonged in one. Yes, it would be nice to have a man like John.

But how could one persuade a prince to love a pauper… with nothing more to offer than the possibility of raising another man's child?

Chapter Ten

John slowly shut the door, and rested his head against it. His mind reeled from all he had overheard. Drawn to the women's voices, he thought the topic of conversation may have been the choices for the night's supper – or some other mundane matter. The last thing he had expected was to learn that Mercedes was...

Pregnant.

He straightened back up and gradually backed away from the door. He turned, walked to the bed and plopped down. Too many questions rolled through his mind, along with too many feelings.

What was it she had said? If she really was with child, then it was because of an attack.

John gritted his teeth. His fists clenched. The urge to strike out at someone – anyone – coursed through him. He'd known enough scoundrels for a lifetime, but he'd never felt as much anger as he did at the moment. Worse, he didn't know which was the real reason. Did he hate the man who had done this to Mercedes because he had violated her?

Or am I upset because she might be carrying his child?

John pulled off his hat and tossed it onto the bed beside him. He buried his head into the palms of his hands, but there was no way to shield himself from the cold, hard facts.

Lord, what am I supposed to do now?

He didn't want to just give up on the idea of getting Mercedes out of Jericho. He owed her at least that much for helping him spring Catalina and Matthew. Besides, he couldn't do that anyway. There was something between them – something he felt the first time he set eyes on her.

Still, there was this other matter. Could he be a father to a child that wasn't his? John let out a heavy sigh.

He just couldn't say.

John lifted his head. He scanned the room, his eyes landing on the Bible that lay on the small stand beside his bed.

A scripture came to mind, though he couldn't remember exactly. "First of John…"

He flipped the book open and thumbed through the pages until reaching the appropriate scripture.

"But whoso hath the world's goods and sees his brother in need and closes his heart against him, how dwelleth the love of God in him?"

John closed the book with resolve. He would not shut Mercedes out if she showed him interest, but allow things to take their natural course.

Well, as much as possible.

He laid the Bible back down as he stood, crossing the room to examine his earlier purchases. He didn't know which color was Mercedes favorite, but wanted to give her the opportunity to wear something other than the saloon outfit. The horrible crimson sash around her waist declared to the world that she belonged to Belmonte, and he wanted to get rid of it. To burn it and make his own declaration.

He wouldn't share her with anyone ever again.

A knock at the door forced John out of his thoughts.

"Come in."

"I can't." Mercedes muffled voice sounded from the other side. "My hands are full."

John walked across the room and pulled the door open to find her with a large wooden tray in hand.

"What in the world? Looks like you prepared a small feast." John's mouth watered at the smell of food that wafted towards him. Boiled chicken, rice, beans, tortillas… and a few other items he could only guess were vegetables of some sort. "Please, do come in."

He stepped aside and waved her in. He purposely left the door partially open, then quickly rushed over to the stand. He moved the Bible over.

"There you go. You can set that down right here."

Mercedes nodded agreeably. "I thought you might be a little hungry."

Careful (as though concerned she would disturb his Bible) she maneuvered the tray until it sat cattycornered from the good book.

"Yes, ma'am." He nodded. "I could eat two whole cows iffin you grew 'em."

Mercedes drew her lips together in a tight smile, but then her lips parted with a rich, throaty laugh. She tried hiding it behind one hand. "Cows aren't grown!"

"Yes, ma'am. I know." John gave her a wide grin. "I was just funnin' you is all."

Mercedes laughed again. She picked up a plate and began dishing out the food onto it. "You talk funny."

John accepted the dish with one hand, the other pointing to himself with feigned surprise. "*Me?* Are you kidding?"

He sat on the edge of the bed and picked up a tortilla. Would she take the bait he set out?

"I'm still trying to figure out some word your friend, Fea, used earlier today."

"Ah, yes. Fea." Mercedes picked up a mug and filled it. She handed him the milky mixture. Then boldly sat beside him on the bed. "I heard what happened today. That's one of the reasons I brought you the meal. My way of saying gracias for helping a friend."

Her gaze grew soft, and a slow blink made him suddenly aware of every lash on those almond orbs. He felt a small tug and began to lean

forward, but realized what he was doing when he
saw those pretty eyes grow wide.

John jerked upright again, heat rushing to
his face. If he had the tongue for it, he could have
cursed himself for the embarrassment his face
surely showed. He knew it to be true when he
finally glanced back up and saw her mouth form a
pretty 'o' almost as wide as her eyes.

"Sure as shootin' I'm redder than a
tomato."

"No, you're not." Mercedes gave him a
playful smile. "More like a baby tomato just
starting to bloom."

"Why, you little minx!"

Mercedes let out a laugh. "I don't even
know what that means!"

"Well, then. That makes two of us."

"What?" She looked confused. "You don't
know what 'minx' means either?"

"Oh, no. I know what *that* word means."
He took a bite of his food, purposely stalling a
little. "I know what that word means just fine. The
word I was speaking on is the one that girl, Fea,
taught me. And I actually do know what it *means*.
I just don't know how to say it."

"Well, what is it?"

"Pany… pany." He set his food down and
leaned over. "You know. This thing here."

He reached over and tugged on her head
wrap. Her hands quickly flew to her head.

"No!"

John froze.

Mercedes took a ragged breath; frantic hands fiddled with the pañuelo.

"Well, girl." He let out a tired sigh. "I can't make you do anything you don't want to."

His hat still sat on the bed. John slowly reached around her for it. Mere inches away, he glanced up at her.

"I sure do wish you'd trust me, though."

He slowly pulled back, and placed the hat on his head, then stood and shook his legs out. He stopped and turned to look at her once more. With nothing more to say, he touched the brim of his hat to bid her goodbye and walked towards the door.

"Wait."

John turned back to find Mercedes standing beside the bed, head hanging. Her fingers slowly unknotted the bandana and pulled it away from her head.

The braid fell to the floor.

Mercedes stared at John, a mix of emotions portrayed in her eyes. For himself, he didn't know what to feel. First it was a bit of shock and dismay. He remembered how lovely she had looked the first time, hair cascading down to her shoulders. Now stringy wisps of hair mingled with small, uneven curls all around her head. He knew this wasn't something of her own choosing. His fists clenched, anger coursing through him.

"Well?" She demanded, her soft voice nearly cracking. Tears filled her eyes.

"Oh, darling." He rushed over to Mercedes and embraced her, his strong arms completely engulfing her. He wished he could have shielded her from the harsh mistreatment she had suffered. "I'm so sorry this happened to you. Why didn't you tell me?"

He pulled away and looked down at her, but she hung her head.

"Because I know how ugly I look." A small sob escaped. "I didn't want you to know it, too."

"Aw, honey." He hugged her again, then pulled back. A hand on each shoulder, he gave her a reassuring squeeze. She refused to look up, though. So he curled a finger under her chin, and gently lifted her face. Her sad, wet eyes met his.

"I don't care how you look."

Her soft, dreamy gaze drew him in. He leaned forward, gently pulling her face closer to his until he found her yielding lips. Warmth spread through him, his mind turning hazy as her supple body melted into his. He kissed her once more, deeper than the first time, then suddenly pulled back.

"Whew!" He let out a slow exhale and took a step back, removing his hat to fan himself. "I think I just better stand over here for a minute, or we're liable to get into trouble."

Mercedes giggled, but quickly recovered. "Sorry about that."

"Oh, no." John shook the hat at her. "Don't you go apologizing. Ain't nothing for you to be sorry about. Truth be told, I don't want you to think I'm trying to take advantage of you."

The smile fled from her face. Her tone turned serious. "I could never think that of you, John."

He studied her for a long moment.

"Good. I'm glad to hear that." He pushed the Stetson back onto his head. "I want you to feel like you can tell me anything, Mercedes. You hear me? Anything at all."

She hesitated, then nodded.

They stood there, staring at one another. Did she understand what he was suggesting? Was his suggestion too subtle?

He waited, hoping she would offer up the real secret she was hiding.

Her mouth parted as if to speak, but then her gaze darted past him. He turned and looked over his shoulder.

Again?

"Yes, Doña Maria?"

"I'm sorry, John, but you must come outside."

"Outside?"

"Sí, señor. Don Belmonte wishes to speak with you."

"He's *here*?"

"Sí, señor." She nodded emphatically. "He is here, right now. I have not let him in yet, because I did not want him finding you both in the same room and get the wrong idea. But I cannot keep him on the porch for long."

John looked over at Mercedes and she rushed past him.

"I'll be in the kitchen."

John didn't respond. Instead, he looked at Doña Maria and gave her a terse nod. She turned, closing the door as she left.

Hands on his hips, John looked around the room one time. His eyes landed on the Bible.

"Lord, I don't know what your plan is." He thought about all the anguish Mercedes had suffered. Her choppy hair, the horrific rape… the possible outcome from it. The sound of his grinding teeth sounded in his head. He dug his hands into his pockets with the hope that would keep them off his pistol.

"Help me, Lord. Please help me to not go out there and kill that man."

Chapter Eleven

Mercedes worked the pestle as hard as she could. The familiar action of grinding the heavy utensil brought little satisfaction. All she could think of was the fact that Belmonte was only one room away from her. After almost a week of being a free woman – well, *feeling* like one anyway – there he was, ready to take her back to Jericho.

She stopped pounding the herbs and strained to hear what was being said in the sala. However, the voices sounded muffled and she could only guess that they were standing on the far side of the room.

Be brave.

The thought scared her a little. Was she once again ready to face the man who had inflicted so much cruelty on her?

She was filled with the sudden urge to cross herself in a silent prayer of protection. But fought it. She wasn't about to believe the make believe of a God she gave up long ago. She was scared, but not *that* scared. Right? Right.

Mercedes laid the pestle on the counter beside the mortar. Head high, she took a fortifying breath and marched into out of the kitchen…

And right into Belmonte.

"Ah, there she is!" He slowly stepped forward. "How are you enjoying your vacation, amor?"

She cringed at the sound of the pet name and glanced away from him. The room was crowded with a small handful of his men – one of them Mocha. He grinned like a fat cat that had just stolen the cow's milk. Meanwhile, the doña looked like she had eaten a handful of limes, her face a sour frown.

She looked away from them both, choosing to focus on John instead. His strong poker face gave her renewed strength.

"Have you grown dumb, girl? Forget that I like a quick answer?" Belmonte raised a hand. "Perhaps you need a little reminding."

John's hand moved to his gun, and Mercedes quickly shook her head. It wouldn't do any good with Mocha and the other men standing right there.

"Forgive me, Señor Belmonte. I am just overwhelmed by your presence."

The man's hand slowly dropped. His eyes dragged over her body and she could feel him mentally undressing her. She shivered.

"Cold, amor?" Belmonte wrapped his arms around her. Her mouth went dry as his hands deliberately traveled down her body. "Mmm. I forgot how good you felt."

Memories of pretending to enjoy unwelcomed advances flooded her mind. She felt as dark as those midnight exploits.

"Did you also forget how to greet me, amor?" He whispered in her ear then began trailing kisses down the side of her neck.

Bile rose in her throat, a burning sensation that filled her nose and wet her eyes. Her hands turned to fists. Ready to strike, she began to raise one when she felt a familiar hand grip her wrist.

"Adolfo!" Mercedes's surprise of the doña drawing her away was surpassed by the idea that she would use his given name. "How dare you come into my home and disrespect me. Take your men and go at once."

Belmonte glared at the woman.

"Don't tell me what to do, mujer. You're no longer my wife. Remember?"

Mercedes gasped.

Doña Maria stepped forward, a finger pointed at Belmonte. "And whose fault is that? I remember far too well. Do you?"

He swiped away her hand. "No me enseñales."

The woman defied him. She again pointed, this time poking his chest. "Do you remember, viejo, the whore who was pregnant with *your* child?"

Belmonte grabbed her hand and squeezed. "At least she wasn't a barren bruja."

"That's where you're wrong," she whispered. "I was never barren. I just didn't want to risk having a son who would turn out like you."

He glared at her. "You lie."

She shook her head. "No… but I wish I did."

"You lie!"

He hastily turned to the coffee table and kicked it over, then rushed across the room.

"No! Don't!"

It was as if he didn't hear Maria's cries. He grabbed hold of a wood wardrobe lined with Televera plates, and pulled it over. The plates crashed to the ground.

"Stop it! Stop!" Mercedes ran up behind Belmonte. She pounded on his back with both fists. "You're ruining everything!"

Belmonte turned and grabbed hold of her arms. They stared at each other for a long moment.

He looked so old. Much older than Mercedes had ever recalled him looking when she was at Jericho. And if she thought on it hard enough, she could imagine him being just as old or older than Doña Maria – who stood off to the side, fervently praying in Spanish.

Belmonte flung Mercedes across the room and she stumbled into John.

"Hey, now!" John protectively wrapped an arm around her, his free hand drawing his gun at the same time Mocha drew his own.

"Both of you put your guns away," Belmonte demanded.

"If it's all the same to you, I think I'll keep a hold of mine," John replied.

"Why?" Belmonte smirked. "Do you really think you'd get off more than a shot before one of my men gunned you down?"

Mercedes scanned the room. Belmonte was right. John was outnumbered four to one. He'd never be able to take them all out at once.

She reached a hand out and lightly touched his arm. He glanced down at her. She shook her head, hoping to convince him that now was not the time.

He gradually lowered his gun.

"Así es!" Belmonte crowed as if he had just won some grand fight. "You made the right choice, friend. Much safer for you this way. Besides, we should not fight seeing as we're going to be family soon."

"Mister, I don't know what you're talking about, but I'm fairly certain I'm no kin of yours. Never will be."

"Oh, I'm *fairly certain* you will be." A wicked grin stretched across Belmonte's ugly face.

Mercedes shuddered.

What did he mean about them becoming family?

John shifted, his stance widening. He unwrapped his arm from Mercedes and crossed them in front of his chest.

"Let me know when you feel inclined to enlighten me as to *how* that's gonna' happen."

"Simple." Belmonte shrugged. "You will marry my daughter."

Mercedes gasped.

Daughter?

"But you—you don't have one." She felt as though a heavy ball had dropped into the pit of her stomach. Who could Belmonte be referring to?

"Of course I do. Didn't you just hear my *wife*? I left her when the other woman became pregnant."

"You did not leave," interjected Doña Maria. "I threw you out!"

Belmonte ignored her.

"Like I was saying. I *do* have a daughter." He stared down Mercedes. "I call her Guadalupe, but you know her better as La Fea."

The words washed over her like cold water. Her friend – the girl she practically helped raise – was Belmonte's daughter?

It suddenly all made sense. The rule that she was not available to men. Her ability to talk to Belmonte any which way she pleased. The permission to freely walk about town while Mercedes had to earn it. Why, even her beggar look had probably been a ploy!

Mercedes felt faint and the world give way beneath her.

"Whoa, now!" John caught her right as her knees had buckled. He helped straighten her back up, then turned to Belmonte. "And just what makes you think I'd marry that girl?"

"Well, you saved her this morning. And from two of your own."

John bristled. "First off, I believe there's only two kinds of people in this world. The good ones that do what's right, and the bad ones that don't. So you can swallow that whole 'two of your own' nonsense. Second, I'd like to consider myself one of the good ones come judgment day. So I only did what I thought Jesus would do. Don't mean I'm in love with your daughter."

Belmonte waved the comment off. "Didn't say that you were."

"Then what makes you so confident that I'd marry that girl?"

"I think you would do it for her." Belmonte nodded at Mercedes. "The way you have wrapped your arms around her, trying to protect her. Oh, yes. I bet you would do almost anything for her. I can tell these things, you know."

The sinking feeling Mercedes felt dissipated, replaced instead with fire coursing within.

"Don't think I'll let you coerce a friend of mine into doing something so… so… tan loca!" She spat the words out, feeling almost as crazy as the idea itself. "Threaten me all you want. I don't care! I will never ask John to do what you say."

"Threaten you?" Belmonte feigned innocence. "On the contrary, amor. I was going to free you."

Mercedes cocked her head in disbelief.

"What are you talking about?"

"Well, it's quite simple. John marries my little Lupe, and I let you walk right out of Jericho. North, south… wherever you want to go."

She felt confused. "But why?"

Belmonte's face hardened. "Because you're no use to me anymore. You are a traitor. La Malinche. My patrons don't want you, and I've already had you. Plus, there's the issue of what exactly I should do with Lupita. I don't want her growing up in a saloon – never did. And after what happened today? Now I know the best thing to do would be to marry her off. There was always the problem of who to choose, though. Every man that comes through the cantina is a drunkard, gambler, abusive… good as patrons, bad as husbands."

"Until John," Mercedes whispered.

"Exactly!" Belmonte clapped his hands enthusiastically. "Riding into Mexico like a white knight. Ah, yes, my friend. I saw you coming a mile away! And, now look! You'll have the chance to save *two* women for the price of one."

Mercedes swallowed hard. How could this be happening? Not even an hour ago, she was wrapped in John's embrace – the touch of his smooth lips on hers as she shared a terrible secret with him. Now this?

She glanced up to John, hoping he'd have some sort of answer out of all this mess. However, his eyes were locked on Belmonte.

"How long do I have to decide," he asked.

"The wedding is tomorrow at noon."

Chapter Twelve

Both women sat on the sofa. John knew they were watching him, but he couldn't stop pacing the small room they had just finished cleaning. Belmonte had given him this one night to "get the fire out" of his system, and to "enjoy" Mercedes now so he'd be faithful once married.

The man's moral compass certainly isn't pointing in the right direction.

John shook his head at the vulgar idea of bedding a woman before marrying her. Not that he hadn't before. However, his walk with Christ had changed all that. He couldn't possibly imagine himself with Mercedes without first saying…

John stopped pacing.

He let out a whoop and clapped his hands, startling both the women. They stared at him, shock painted on their faces.

"I got it! Hallelujah, I got it!"

"What is it, John?" Excitement laced Mercedes's voice as she stood. "What do you have?"

John sobered up.

"We get married."

Mercedes silently stared at him, mouth hanging open. A mix of emotions played on her face, and he mentally kicked himself for not asking for her hand the proper way.

"Look, Mercedes. It's like this." John reached out and took her hands into his. "I know we don't love each other – not yet anyway. But maybe that'll come later. I mean, there's no denying there's *something* between us. In the meantime, getting hitched solves half our problem. I can't marry Belmonte's daughter if I'm already married to you."

Mercedes released his hands. It was her turn to pace the room.

"But what about your horse?"

"I've been thinking about that, too." John snapped his fingers, then pointed at her. "We steal her back."

"No manches." Mercedes looked at him with disbelief. "How are we going to do that? They'll see us coming a mile away!"

"No they won't." John smiled triumphantly. Confidence oozed from every inch of him. "Not with the plan I have in mind."

Mercedes let out a disheartened sigh.

"That still doesn't solve the first problem. How are we going to get married? We need to find someone who is willing to do it, and I don't think el Padre Carlomango is going to be of much assistance. He does pretty much whatever Belmonte pays him to do."

John thought back to when he first met the clergyman. He wasn't surprised at all to hear he was in Belmonte's pocket. The man had left John with some serious misgivings.

Doña Maria finally stood.

"What about Padre Emmanuel?"

"Nah. That won't work. Even the Father didn't know where the… Father… had gone to."

"Claro qué no!" Doña Maria chuckled. "Padre Emmanuel is in hiding. Only a select few of us actually know where he is."

Mercedes turned to the older woman.

"And you just happen to know where that is?"

"Of course I do!" Doña Maria puffed out her chest with pride, tapping it with her thumb. "*I* am the one who hid him."

"*You*?" Both John and Mercedes chorused at the same time. They stared at one another, awestruck. John tore his eyes away from her and back to the doña.

"I thought Father Emmanuel was excommunicated."

Doña Maria waved the idea away.

"Anyone who saw those papers from the Vatican could tell they were as fake as a homemade peso. In fact, I wouldn't be surprised if the new Padre himself is a fake. The way he rode up to the church accompanied by some of Adolfo's men? Pfffth."

She stuck her tongue out and they laughed.

Mercedes sobered. "To hear you call that man by his first name, and to think that you were—"

"Ya sé, nena. Ya sé." The woman hung her head. "It's a fact I'll have to live with for the rest of my life."

"And that was when you—"

Doña Maria sadly nodded her head. She didn't say a word, but she didn't need to. Despite the fact that Mercedes hadn't yet confessed to possibly being with child, John knew that the women were referring to whatever drink could help her end a pregnancy.

He kept a shudder at bay, and opted to change the subject.

"So you do know where Father Emmanuel is?"

"Sí, señor."

"Good. Then you can take us to him."

Mercedes let out an exasperated sigh. "I don't want to be the heavy shoe, but let's not forget the details. *How* are we going to get to Padre Emmanual? Don't forget. There are now *two* guards outside."

John began pacing again.

She was right. A second man had been left behind to ensure that neither Mercedes nor John could reach American soil. One chap he could've snuck up on and taken out on his own. Two? That made things a bit more difficult.

"Wait a minute. Didn't you say you've got some sort of plant that makes people sleep?"

"Yes. I have La Durmida." Mercedes confirmed. "It's a lot like Belladonna, and it would work. But let me tell something to you. Those men out there are not tea drinking men."

"Nah. You're right." John kicked the floor with the toe of his boot. "Too bad I'm not a drinking man. They'd probably take a glass of whiskey if I had it. Then we could add some of that Durmida stuff into it."

"How about tequila?"

They both turned to Doña Maria. She looked at them with innocence on her face.

"What?" She asked indignantly. "It's good for cleaning cuts – not to mention entertaining important guests."

John cracked a smile. "Yeah, well, considering we got two chaps out front who hold the key to liberty, they're pretty important. Who knows? They might just be willing to celebrate a man's last night of freedom."

"I'll get the bottle."

"And I'll brew the tea!" Mercedes whispered with excitement.

John chuckled as both women sped off into different directions, and he himself headed for the bedroom. Part one of the plan was well underway.

"Now for part two." He murmured, eyeing the new cloth he had bought for Mercedes.

"Why did you separate it?" John hesitantly accepted the small mug of tequila Mercedes had prepared. "You know I don't drink this stuff."

Mercedes let out a frustrated sigh. She could appreciate – and even accept – his personal beliefs, but did he have to be so obstinate about them?

"John, do you really think those men out there are going to trust you enough to drink whatever you hand them without seeing you drink it, too?

"Guess you've got a point there."

"Then let's get to it." She handed him the bottle. "The sun sits low. That means we have about half an hour to dark – exactly the time needed for the Durmida to kick in."

"Right! Then we can hightail it out of here. In the meantime, you and Doña Maria get started on that project I gave you."

"Yes, sir!"

Mercedes gave John a pretend salute.

"You little spitfire." He laughed, lightly chucking her chin with his fist. Then he turned, bottle and mug in hand, and headed out the front door.

"Ready, hija?"

Mercedes turned to find the doña's hands full of bright colored clothes.

"Sí." Mercedes sat on the sofa and picked up a sewing needle. "We have to hurry."

"Wait." Doña Maria sat across from her. "Things will go much smoother with three."

Mercedes looked at the woman as if she had gone mad.

"What are you talking about, Doña? John is outside. That leaves just the two of us."

"No, hija. We are never alone." The woman held out a long wooden rosary with a cross on one end; a medallion with the Virgin of Guadalupe dangling beside it. "Take this."

"Ay, qué no, Doña." Mercedes pushed the withered hand away. "I can't."

"Yes, you can."

The woman leaned forward and looped the rosary over her head. It hung around Mercedes like a necklace. She fingered one smooth bead, then wrapped her fist around the rosary.

"Too many men have forced me to give away my body." She released the beads and her voice hardened. "I won't let one take away my mind."

She looked back up to find Doña Maria wiping away a tear.

"Ay, hija. I understand why you feel that way, but it breaks my heart to hear it. How can you feel He is trying to take *anything* away from you? Look at what he's already given you!"

"Given me?!" Mercedes voice raised a decimal. She ran a hand through her course hair, her voice thick with disgust as she spoke. "A nearly shaved head and maybe even an unwanted baby."

She buried her face in her hands and cried loud, wretched sobs that shook her body.

"Shhh. Ya." Doña Maria wrapped her arms around her. "Don't cry, mi'ja. It isn't as bad as all that. You'll see. God is good, and all children are a blessing from Him. If you find you are indeed with child, then know there could be no better woman to mother this babe. And to think! You won't even have to do it alone, because He also gave you John."

Mercedes sniffed.

She wiped the back of her hand across her moist face, digesting all that the woman had said. It all sounded good in theory. There was just one problem.

"I still haven't told John the truth," she confessed.

"Well, hija, you better get to it." Doña Maria picked up a sewing needle and began working. "After all, it's like the Bible says. 'The truth shall set you free.'"

Mercedes picked up her own needle to hem the opposite side of the royal blue cloth. A myriad of thoughts ran through her mind.

Would telling the truth really make things better? Or would the truth run John off? Should she share with him the details of her attack… or just drink the tea and get on with her life?

Chapter Thirteen

John quietly shut the door. The better part of an hour had passed, and one of the men still hadn't been effected as he had hoped. He looked down at the nearly empty tequila bottle.

"So?" Mercedes whispered behind him. "Are they asleep?"

John turned to find her looking up at him, eyes eager with anticipation. He loathed the task of having to tell her the truth.

"Unfortunately, no."

Her face fell, the light in her eyes dying as she hung her head. He wrapped one arm around her small frame, pulling her close. He gave her a reassuring squeeze.

"That doesn't mean we can't still go through with the plan." He released her and handed over the bottle. "It just means we'll have to modify it a little."

"What do you mean?" She crossed the room and sat the bottle on the table.

"Well, the one guy did drink a fair deal of the tequila. I came back in when he started nodding off. However, that Mocha fella is still kicking pretty good."

"How much did he drink?"

"Just a couple of sips." John hesitated. "I think he got a little suspicious when he didn't see me drinking, too."

"You didn't drink?" Mercedes looked at him with disbelief.

"No." John confessed. He hung his head as he slowly approached her. "I pretended to be sipping it, then tossed it out when no one was looking."

Mercedes slapped her forehead.

"Oh, John." She groaned. "Trust me. He was looking."

"You think so?"

"I know so." She crossed her arms in front of her chest with a huff. "You don't get a reputation like 'Mocha Oreja' just by chance, or because you know the right people. You have to prove yourself ruthless. One way of doing that is by seeing everything while saying nothing. The other is by creatively killing people. I guarantee Mocha saw you… and he probably has all kinds of twisted things running through his mind right now."

"Then we're just gonna' have to outwit him." John's resolve strengthened. "I mean, that's all there is to it."

"Alright." Mercedes waved John off. "Move out of my way."

"Move out of your way? For what?"

"I'm going to go out there and distract him. Then you can come out and bop him on the head… or whatever it is you do."

John began to step aside.

"Hey, wait a minute now." He stopped, a niggling thought playing with his mind. "What exactly do you mean when you say 'distract him?' Best not be the kind of distracting that would put a smile on a man's face."

"You mean this kind?" Mercedes gave him a little shimmy, and his mouth dropped open.

"Relax," she said with a smile. "I'm not in that line of work anymore. Remember? Besides, you're about to make an honest woman out of me."

"And don't you forget it." Laughter tinged his voice, but he knew that for all the playful banter, they were both as nervous as a sinner in church for Sunday service. A match against Mocha and a marriage "in name only," weren't the most ideal situations to be in.

He cleared his throat and his mind. "So what exactly do you plan on doing?"

"I'm going to act like I'm heading back to Jericho with the hope that he'll follow me."

"And if he doesn't?"

"I'm betting he will – especially if he calls me out and I ignore him. He hates that! He can't tolerate being snubbed by a woman one bit. And definitely not by a so-called Malinche. So he's sure to follow me. As soon as he does, you do your thing."

John thought about her plan for a moment.

"Alright." He agreed. "I think it'll work. Only if you go out the back and walk around the side of the house, though. It'll be easier to surprise him that way than if I were to come straight out the front."

"Esta bien." Mercedes headed towards the back door. "Let's do it."

"What about me?"

They both turned. Doña Maria stood in the entrance of her bedroom, arms wrapped around a small bundle.

"I could hit him in the head or something." John chuckled.

First, she has tequila. Now she wants to get in on the action.

"I think it might be a better idea if you stay inside, and let us handle the coup." John pointed to the wad she carried. "Just don't forget that right there, or we can kiss our escape goodbye."

"You can count on me," she assured him.

"Good." John looked at Mercedes. "Ready?"

Her eyes were wide with fright, but she nodded all the same. John didn't know whether to hug her, or slap her on the back. He had known men with less fortitude than she displayed. The way she had stood up to Belmonte, and was now going to lure Mocha away from his post? The gal had grit!

He followed her out the back, both their bodies side by side as they crept along the house.

When they got to the corner, Mercedes slowly peered around it, then quickly pressed herself against the wall again. Her breath quickened. John grabbed hold of her hand and gave it a little squeeze for reassurance. She squeezed his hand in return, then released it and walked off into the moonlit street.

She walked quickly, and approached the neighboring house within seconds. However, there still was no sign of Mocha.

John began to worry. What if they were wrong? What if Mocha had only been instructed to guard *him*? Maybe they didn't really care anymore what happened to Mercedes. So long as Belmonte could marry off his daughter, then that was all that really mattered.

Maybe they always knew she'd return to Jericho… just like she did the first time I offered to get her out.

Just as the seed of doubt started to take root in his mind, he saw a second shadow on the street.

"Adónde vas?"

Head high and shoulders straight, Mercedes continued walking.

"Hey!" Mocha stepped into sight. His tone turned ferocious. "WHERE ARE YOU GOING?"

One hand slid to his waist, and John saw the flash of something silver beneath his fingers.

A knife!

John jumped out from his hiding spot. He rushed the man, ready to tackle him from behind. Mocha raised the stiletto…

Then quickly turned.

John dodged to the side, but the knife still found its mark. He let out a scream as it embedded in his arm, swinging him around. He grabbed his arm as he fell to the ground.

"No!" Mercedes cried. She ran towards him.

"Stop!" He barely commanded before Mocha dove at him, grabbing at the knife. He twisted it.

The sheriff screamed again.

Pain shot down to his fingertips, and up to his brain. He instinctively balled his fist, then swung with his good arm. Bright red exploded from his assailant's nose. The force knocked him off.

John sprang to his feet. He withdrew his pistol just as Mocha stood. The man dove at him again, knocking the gun from his hand. It bounced along the road, out of John's reach.

Mocha pulled the knife out of John's arm. He let out another cry and raised a fist again. The Mexican blocked it.

"I'm gonna' show you how I earned my name," he crowed.

Leaning forward, he brought the knife close to John's ear. The tip grazed his earlobe.

John squirmed, bent his legs, and planted his boots firmly into the ground. He tried to buck the man off, but Mocha held on. The blade momentarily swung away from John.

He drove the knife at John as a shot sounded.

Mocha's face contorted with pain. His arm dropped to his side, the knife dangling between his fingertips. He stared at John, his eyes filled with an unwanted knowing, then slowly fell forward.

John caught the man and pushed him away. His heavy body flopped onto the dirt road. He moved his mouth as if to speak, but only a gurgle sounded. Red tinged his lips and his eyes glazed over.

John stood and slowly dragged his eyes away from the dead man.

Mercedes stared at the lifeless body, both hands still gripping the pistol. John slowly approached her.

"Hey, girl." His voice was a soft whisper. Her wild eyes met his. He raised his good arm and offered his hand. "It's alright. It's all over now."

She slowly blinked, then glanced down to the gun in her shaky hands.

"John?" Her voice cracked. She dropped the gun, and large tears sprang up. "I just ki—"

"Shhh." He closed the gap between them. "I know, I know. Don't you even think about that right now."

He wrapped his good arm around her.

"But I... I just—"

"—did exactly what you had to do." He spoke into her short, soft hair and breathed her in. Her scent reminded him of a garden in full bloom. His mind grew foggy, and he could've stood there – lost in the moment forever. But her hand ran down his wounded arm.

"Aw, woman." He let out a groan.

"John!" She gasped and released him. She studied the tear in his shirt. "We have to get you inside right now so I can tend to that."

He gently pulled back. "For as much I'd like to get a bit of your healing touch, I'm afraid that'll have to wait."

"Alright. I'll go get Doña Maria."

She raced back across the street, bounding up the steps and disappearing into the house. John walked back over to where Mocha laid.

The man had been a real work of evil, but even he desired a proper burial. Unfortunately, there wasn't any time for that at the moment. Still, it wasn't like he could just leave the man lying in the middle of the road. What if someone happened by?

John grabbed a hold of the man with one arm and dragged him off to the side of the house.

"There. That'll keep you for a bit."

He paced back around to the front only to find Mercedes had reappeared. She ran up to him, the bottle of tequila in her hands.

"Where's the doña?"

"She's coming. Now give me your arm."

Mercedes grabbed his hand and stretched his arm out.

"Oh, I don't know about that. I'm thinking that stuff's likely to burn hotter than—"

She splashed the alcohol onto his arm.

John inhaled sharply. A somewhat unpleasant slang sprung to his lips. He bit his tongue to keep it in check.

"Bless the night. I'll be happy to see morning."

"Yes." Mercedes tied a clean cloth around the wound. "Hopefully on the other side of the border."

"With a new bride *and* my horse in tow."

Doña Maria approached them, still carrying the bundle. "We better find el Padre if you want to make that happen!"

John took Mercedes's hand and placed it in the crook of his good arm. He looked back at the old woman. He imagined what it would've been like to have a mother, and decided that he wouldn't have minded having one like Doña Maria.

He nodded at her.

"Lead the way, Ma."

The woman beamed at him, then stood a little taller and marched down International Boulevard as if she owned it.

Chapter Fourteen

The houses grew farther apart, the vast desert dark behind them. A chill crawled up Mercedes's spine, and the hair at the nape of her neck prickled.

"Are you sure you know where you're going?" She asked the doña. "Not too much more and we'll be in el campo."

"Where did you think we were going?"

"We're going to *el campo*?" Mercedes asked with disbelief. "How will we get back in time?"

"Don't worry. You'll make it."

John cleared his throat.

"Uh, what exactly do you mean by el campo? Sounds kind of rural." He glanced around. "Looks it, too."

"That's exactly what it is." Mercedes confirmed. She turned her attention back to Doña Maria. "Maybe this wasn't such a good idea. I think you should take us back."

"No! Let's stick to the plan." John urged.

"But why?" She pulled her arm out of his and they both stopped walking. "Couldn't we just sneak across to the other side? I mean, look! There it is right now."

"But with everything going on at the moment – especially after that little battle y'all had with each other – the army isn't gonna' let you saunter on over as big as you please. In fact, they've got soldiers at the customs crossing now. So the only way you're getting in is if you're married to an American." John started walking again, murmuring under his breath. "Besides, I can't leave without Abby."

Mercedes firmly planted her hands on her hips. "Wait a minute! Are you doing all of this for a stupid horse?"

"What?" John stopped.

She could barely make out his features in the pale moonlight, but she could guess what he looked like by the sound of his voice. And it told her that she was as loca as she felt, walking across the desert to find an ex-communicated priest.

He took a few steps closer to her, and his hardened features became clear.

"Now you listen here." He wagged a finger at her, his voice as stern as his steely eyes. "There is no such thing as a stupid horse. And that goes double true for Abby. You hear? The two of you are gonna' have to get along."

Mercedes crossed her arms and frowned.

"I'm serious, girl." John insisted. "I'm getting my horse back one way or another. Now if Belmonte catches me in the act and I'm already married, then there won't be much more he can do except shoot me. And who knows? Maybe he would. Maybe he wouldn't. Either way, there's no man on the face of God's good earth, coming along and taking a horse from the grandson of a Comanche chief without some kind of reckoning. It just can't be. Do you understand?"

Mercedes dropped her arms to her side.

"Yes."

"Good."

Mercedes let out her pent up breath as John turned back around and stalked away. She watched him for a few seconds, then ran to catch up.

"Well, I guess there's something to be said about a man who loves his horse as much as you love yours."

"Oh, yeah? What's that?"

"At least you're loyal."

John wrapped his good arm around her shoulders. "Well, as long as you don't mind being the 'other lady.'"

Mercedes guffawed and John chuckled.

"Aw, I'm just funnin' you." He pulled her closer. "You'll always be more important to me than any horse – even Abby. But she's important, too. Okay? For starters, she's the only ride we've got to get back to North Carolina."

"Is that where we're going?"

"Yes, ma'am. I've already talked to Matt and Cat, and they've said we can stay with them until we find our legs."

"You mean, Catalina is in… What did you call it again?"

"North Carolina."

"That's right." A cool breeze brushed against her bare arms. She instinctively huddled closer to him. "It's been a long while since I've been out walking at night. I forgot how cold it gets in the desert at night."

"Oh, well, you'll be in for something surprising when we get Stateside. They get snow during the winter months."

"Really? I've never seen snow. Heard a little about it, though. People say it even falls here, in the serros further South. But I don't know if it's entirely true, because I've never been to the mountains."

"Well, you won't have to go to any mountains to see snow once we get back home."

Home.

The way he said it sounded nice. Reassuring. They were going to be married and share their lives together building a home. She could see them in their own house – her tending the garden while he groomed his silly horse. The children –

Mercedes stopped walking.

"What's the matter, darling?"

She looked up at him, the beat of her heart quickening. "John, there's something –"

"There it is." Doña Maria pointed to a small, dilapidated structure in the distance. Mercedes couldn't imagine anyone living there.

"Are you sure, Doña? Half the roof is caved in."

"Sí, nena. That's to make people think there is nothing important going on."

John's hand instinctively moved to his hip. "What do you mean?"

"Come! I'll show you." The woman stepped up to the door and – without even knocking – swung it open. She ushered them in.

"Good grits and gravy! What in the world happened to this place?"

The two of them scanned the one room hovel, dimly lit by the night sky shining in through the missing roof. Shuffling across the dirt floor, they followed Doña Maria in. There was a cold, crumbling fireplace on the far side of the room. A wooden table missing one leg leaned dangerously on its side; the only available chair, splintered.

Mercedes wondered if the old woman was losing her mind.

"You're obviously mistaken, Doña Maria. There's no one here."

"You're right," she agreed. "There's no one here… in *this* room. However, there's sure to be quite a few downstairs."

Downstairs?

John and Mercedes looked at one another, confused, until the woman led them to the fireplace. She leaned in and tapped the back wall of it.

"Go on." She instructed John. "Push."

He stepped forward and did as told. The wall easily gave way, swinging open to reveal a passage of stone steps.

"Alright now. This is a little strange." John ducked to enter. "Mind telling us what's going on here?"

"A revolution!" Doña Maria whispered with excitement.

"What kind of revolution?" Mercedes followed behind them. "And where is that light coming from?"

"Oh, it's always well-lit down below. We don't want any of the Zapatistas to fall and injure themselves."

"Zapatistas? What would they be doing here? We're a long way from Morelos."

"Sí, hija. But we've enlisted a few to help us take back our town."

They reached the bottom of the stairs and found themselves standing in a small room filled with burning candles. They surrounded a statue of the Virgin of Guadalupe.

Doña Maria stopped in front of the statue and crossed herself, then pointed at the only door in the room.

"Through here." She squeezed past John. Balling her fist, she knocked on the thick wood seven times.

The door cracked open, a slender face appearing.

"It's me, Padre."

"Doña Maria?" The priest swung the door open and welcomed them in. "What are you doing here at so late an hour?"

"We've come on a quest!"

"A what?"

The doña introduced John and Mercedes. Within minutes, they had explained their predicament – everything from when John had first been searching for Father Emmanuel at the church, to the run-in with Mocha.

"So will you help us, Padre?" Mercedes pleaded.

"Yeah, will you marry us?" John chimed in.

Father Emmanuel studied them both. He eyed Mercedes a second time.

"You're sure this is what you want to do?"

They both nodded.

"Alright. Then I will marry you." He turned to John. "But know that our customs are a bit different from yours."

"What do you mean?"

"We have very specific traditions that we follow when getting married."

John looked thoughtful.

"Let me ask you something, Padre. Do you believe in God?"

"Claro qué sí! I wouldn't be a priest if I didn't."

"And you believe that Jesus came to earth in order to die for our sins so we could have a chance to be in his kingdom?"

"Of course."

"Well, then, it makes no never mind to me how you go about, so's long it's done right in the eyes of God and man."

"And you, hija? Surely you are agreeable to the arrangement."

Mercedes stared at the priest as though he had spoken a completely foreign language. She suddenly felt like a big fraud. She had spent years of her life blaming God for every bad thing that happened. From the moment the Calendeza's were struck down to the rapes she endured – the last of which she just *knew* left her with child. All of it, *all of it*, had been God's fault. And she had been angry with him – so angry she could scream and cry and spit… and maybe even say some of those foul words the men at Jericho were always throwing around.

"Are you okay, hija?" The priest eyed her suspiciously.

"Oh, she's fine." John interjected. "We got into a little spat just a bit ago about her not *really* playing second fiddle to my horse. It kind of threw a damper on the whole plan for a minute there. But, nope. Everything's good now. Right Mercedes?"

She took a deep breath.

"Can I talk with you for a moment? I mean, alone?" She pointed to the door, indicating that they return to the former room.

"Uh…"

"Hija!" Doña Maria grabbed Mercedes by the shoulders and pulled her close. "We do not have time for this. Now warm those cold feet. Light a fire under them and let's go!"

Mercedes allowed the woman to push her into position, beside John with the priest in front of both of them. Maybe Doña Maria was onto something. Maybe it really was as simple as 'cold feet.' Didn't the doña say that God had given her John?

Could this be His way of trying to show He really does care?

"Seeing as you, Mr. Durbin, do not know the Gloria, we'll just skip that and go right into prayer."

Father Emmanuel bowed his head, and everyone followed suit. As he began to pray, Mercedes realized two things.

One, she really was about to get married to John Durbin, the sheriff who rode into Mexico like some knight out of a storybook.

Two, God had to be real. If he wasn't, then how could she be getting ready to say "I do" and ride into the sunset with her cowboy?

"Amen."

She lifted her head, repeating after el Padre, and realized that to her surprise she really meant it.

Chapter Fifteen

"That was awfully nice of the Padre to loan us his mule."

John tapped the reigns against the against the animal's back, urging it to move a little faster. The buckboard jostled a little harder.

"Yes." Mercedes rocked side to side, her shoulder softly bumping against John. She looked back. Amazingly, Doña Maria had dozed off. Mercedes faced front again, head hanging. Her voice was a soft murmur only loud enough for her husband to hear. "We'll definitely make it back before the cantina closes and everyone passes out."

John noted the hint of sorrow in her voice. It wasn't right for a new bride to be sad on her wedding day – even if the wedding itself wasn't much of one.

Am I being unreasonable?

"Listen." He pulled back on the mule until it stopped. He turned to Maria. "Maybe this isn't such a good idea. I mean, I really do want to go and get Abby. I think she'd be a real asset to us once we're back in the States. Plus, she's my horse. A gift from the town of Abilene for catching a notorious gang of bank robbers. So make no mistake. I really do want her."

He paused and studied her dark brown eyes long enough to lose his train of thought. Overwhelmed by desire, he took her chin between his fingers and gradually pulled her close. Her soft lips greeted his, gently parting as the kiss deepened. She exhaled. Her slow, shaky breath mingled with his, and he knew he could go on kissing her like that for the rest of his life.

Which was why he had to do this.

John cleared his throat and sat back up, trying hard to ignore the smile of satisfaction on his new bride's face.

Whew wee! There's some fire in that gal.

John gave himself a shake.

"Like I was saying, I *do* want Abby." He carefully glanced over at her. His voice grew serious. "But not at the risk of losing you."

Her brows drew together with confusion. "I don't understand. How could you lose me? We're married now. Do you really think I'd choose a place like Jericho over someone like you?"

"That ain't it at all. I *know* you wouldn't choose that kind of life again." His confident declaration brought a smile back to her face. "But what we're about to do will be a little dangerous."

Mercedes shrugged. "Not really. Belmonte said I was free. Right? I'm just going to collect my things. That's all."

Despite her simple explanation, John knew that was *not* all. Sure, she was going to collect her belongings. However, the rest of the plan was for her to find the gate key, while he waited outside to be let in. Talk about dangerous! One wrong move and the results could be downright disastrous.

"Well, if doesn't bother you so much to go back in there, then what's wrong? You looked kinda' sad a minute ago. I thought maybe you were worryin' about the plan."

Mercedes opened her mouth to speak when a rustling noise sounded from behind. They both turned to see Doña Maria roll, reposition herself, and then fall back asleep. They looked back at each other and John mouthed, "*So?*"

Mercedes signaled for him to drive on. He picked up the reigns again, urging the mule forward.

"Listen," she turned sideways in her seat to face him. "I've got something to tell you. Something important. I mean, *really* important. Bigger than anything else I've told you about me or my life. And you might not like me once I tell you what it is."

John schooled his expression, but was pretty sure he already knew what was coming. He gave her an encouraging nod.

"Sounds pretty serious."

"It is."

"Might be a good idea to go ahead and get it out then. Don't you think?"

"Yeah." Mercedes took a deep breath. "I'm pregnant."

She waited for some reaction, but he sat still, eyes still trained on the road.

"I'm sorry." She blurted. Then everything rushed out, a geyser of truth that couldn't be stopped. "I know, I know. I should have told you when we first spoke. I mean, not when we *first* spoke. I wasn't pregnant when you came to the saloon looking for your friends. But some bad things happened after you left, and I had a feeling I was but wasn't too sure if it was definite. So I still didn't say anything when you returned – even though you were so nice and all to get me out of there and over to Doña Maria's house. And then I didn't think it mattered if I said anything, because I wasn't too sure how you felt, and if you didn't feel anything and I was going back to Jericho anyway… Well, then, why embarrass myself? But then I started thinking maybe I really did have a chance to be with you. But who would want a woman carrying another man's child? So I was going to get rid of it, because I have some stuff in my bag to do that. But then I couldn't. I just couldn't… Not even for someone as wonderful as you."

Her voice cracked. She buried her head in her hands. A muffled sob sounded through them.

"Hey, now."

John placed a hand on her back and gently massaged it. He had wanted her to share the truth with him, but hadn't prepared for it to all come out at once. He felt like a real heel for allowing her to go on like that.

She lifted her head and turned to him. "I truly am sorry, John. I'll understand if you don't want me anymore."

"*What?*" John felt as though the wind had been knocked right out of his sails. "Where'd you get a fool idea like that? Of course, I still want you!"

Mercedes swiped at her face, brushing away persistent tears.

"Does that mean you forgive me?"

John let out a sigh.

"Darling, if there's anyone needing forgiveness right now, it's me."

"You? What would you need forgiveness for? You've been nothing but wonderful, and me... Well, I guess you could say I've been a bit difficult."

John gave her a half-smile. "I won't deny that any, but I speak the truth. You don't owe me an apology for anything. Fact is, I owe you one for not 'fessing up that I've known about the youngin.'"

Mercedes mouth dropped open with surprise. "You knew? But how? I've never spoke about it to anyone except..."

"Yeah, and that's exactly when I knew, too." John admitted. "I overhead you telling the doña there about it. Not that I was trying to eavesdrop, mind you. It was an accident, and what I should've done was make my presence known right away. But we were still on shaky terms then, and I didn't want you to suffer more than you already had. So I figured you'd eventually come around and tell me in due time."

Mercedes bit her bottom lip, obviously considering all he had said. She peered up at him again, a hopeful look in her eyes.

"So how do you feel about it?"

It was John's turn to look contemplative. "Honestly? I don't know."

She deflated a little, and he hurried on.

"That is, I'm not saying that I won't take care of the little tyke. I'll claim him as my own and do my best to provide for him – the same as I'll do for you. But if you're asking me how I'll *feel* about it. Well, I can't rightfully say. I'd like to think that I'd treat him the same as I would any one of our other children, though."

He hoped the answer he gave her was good enough. One look confirmed it was.

"Other children?" A playful grin graced her face once again. Her eyes softened. "How many of them were you planning on anyway?"

John whistled. "Shoo, I don't know. As many as the good Lord will give us! I reckon maybe ten will do."

She gasped. "Ten!"

"Yes, ma'am. Why not? Sounds like a good, even number to me. Get me a whole parcel of little cowboys to break the horses we breed."

"We're going to breed horses?"

"Of course. Why do you think I want to return for Abby? She's not just my horse, you know. She's pretty valuable. I find her a good ol' boy to get with, and they'll make a fine colt. Then we'll just keep going until we have one of the finest horse farms North Carolina's ever seen!"

Mercedes laughed.

"I like your vision, but there might be a problem with your plan."

"Oh, yeah? Lay it on me."

"What if you have ten girls?"

John clutched his chest, inhaling sharply. "Whoa, girl! Be careful there. You're liable to give a man a heart attack."

Mercedes laughed again.

John smiled, then pointed in front of them. "Look! There's the house."

Mercedes pointed out the second guard, still asleep out front.

"Yeah, and it looks like everything's still the same."

"Good. That's real good." He pulled on the reigns until the buckboard came to a stop. "Alright. I'm going to jump down and get changed. You wake up Doña Maria for the switch."

"I'm already awake."

John and Mercedes both jumped at the sound of the woman's voice.

"Sorry, Doña." John reached back to help the woman up into the front. "We didn't mean to wake you so abruptly."

"What made you think I was ever asleep?"

"You mean to tell us you were awake the whole time?" The old woman took John's seat as he climbed down. "Why didn't you say anything?"

"What? And give you both honeymoon jitters?" She waved him away. "You two seemed to have a lot to talk about, and I didn't want to get in the way."

John shook his head. The old gal really was something else. He walked around to the opposite side. Mercedes offered up the small bundle they had brought along. He opened it and grabbed the garments from inside. Pushing a hand through one armhole, he pulled the outfit over his head.

"Here." Mercedes handed him a shawl. "Wrap this around your head and shoulders."

John did as instructed. When he was finished, he posed for her approval.

"How do I look?" John twirled, the fabric billowing out around his legs.

"Like the ugliest woman I've ever seen," she laughed.

His mouth fell open. "Hey, now! Don't blame me. I'm not the one who made the dress."

Mercedes giggled again and Doña Maria hushed them both. "Ya se calmen! Maybe you two have forgotten the next stop is Jericho, but I remember full well what Adolfo did to my house earlier. Do not be fooled. He's not someone to mess with!"

"You're right." John sobered up and climbed into the back of the buckboard, laying down to hide. "My apologies."

"Esta bien." Doña Maria accepted the sincerity. "Now don't forget. I won't be there when you two come out. I'm only driving to the end of the road. Mercedes, you will get out and cross the street to Jericho. John, you will head in the opposite direction and wait by the back gate. Then I will go to the border and inform the soldiers to be on the watch for you. Sále?

"Agreed." They echoed and the doña slapped the reigns, driving the buggy until the lights of Jericho came into view. Loud, rowdy music sounded from within.

A few hands stood around out front, smoking and talking while they kept watch. Mercedes leaned back a little.

"Suerte," she whispered over her shoulder.

"Don't need luck," John replied. "Not when you've got God on your side."

"Then we better pray real hard, because we're about to go into the lion's den."

Mercedes climbed down and strolled across the street to the front of the saloon. One of the men tried to stop her, but she raised a hand, mumbling something inaudible to them. They conversed a few seconds longer, then led her into Jericho.

"Go!" Doña Maria whispered to John. He slid out the back of the buckboard and ran across the street, the dress whipping around his ankles until he reached the locked gate.

All the while he muttered a prayer that all would go well. That Mercedes would find the key. That they'd get Stateside in one piece. That he would have enough love to go around for both her… *and* the child she carried.

Chapter Sixteen

"I don't need an escort, chivatos." Mercedes hissed at the two men who accompanied her into Jericho.

"No?" The first man grabbed her arm and swung her around. His face hovered inches away from hers. "Then where are the two you were originally given, and why did they let you come here alone?"

Mercedes yanked her arm out of his grasp. "Like I said, one of them fell asleep. You can go down and check right now if you'd like."

She waved the bait in front of them, but hoped they wouldn't take it. If they really did go down to Doña Maria's house, they might find out what happened to Mocha.

"And the other one, Mocha Orejas?" The second man questioned her. "Where did he run off to?"

"Nowhere!" Mercedes huffed. "He's still at the house."

It wasn't a lie, but anymore questions and she might buckle under pressure. She couldn't afford to tell any tales. Besides trying to start married life out on the right foot, she was a terrible liar anyway.

"And the American?" The first guy asked.

She only shrugged in response and both men laughed.

"Looks like a Malinche like you isn't even good enough for the guerros."

She ignored the crude remark and pushed past both of them.

"Look. Belmonte and the American had a deal. I'm a free woman. Remember? So I'm just going to go upstairs and get my things."

They didn't try to stop her when she marched to the stairs, head held high, but the first one did call after her.

"Sí, Malinche. You go do that. We'll let Belmonte know you're back."

The taunt echoed in her mind as she found the room she once called hers. She turned the knob and entered.

Everything was exactly the same as it had always been. Why? Some of the other girls had to share rooms. Besides, he was sure to have acquired one or two more ladies in the week she'd been away. Why hadn't he given it to any of them?

The answer was obvious. He never had any intention of letting her go.

A shudder ran through Mercedes. She needed to get out of here!

She removed her revolso and laid it on the bed. Quickly scouring the room, she located the items that were worth taking. A hand mirror and brush, a few undergarments, and the Bible that

Catalina had left behind. She laid them all on the shawl, then brought the corners together and tied the fabric into a thick knot.

She slung the bundle over her shoulder, then ran to the door. Gradually opening it, she peered out to ensure there was no one to stop her.

Next stop, La Fea.

Mercedes stepped out of the room and walked to the end of the hall to La Fea's room. Knowing the girl wouldn't have a visitor inside, she didn't even bother knocking.

A girl sat in a rocking chair, her back to the door. She looked out the room's only window, humming.

Mercedes quietly shut the door behind her. "Fea?"

The girl quieted.

Mercedes walked around to face the girl. She dropped the bundle when she saw the girl's face.

"Fea? Why, you're not Fea at all." She fought to find the right words. "Lupita, you're beautiful!"

Color tinged Lupita's cheeks. She dropped her head with embarrassment. "Ay, hermana. Don't go on so."

"How can I not? I've never seen you like this!"

Where once was an unkempt girl with shabby clothes and smudges of dirt on her chin, now stood a clean, young woman with braids in her hair and a pretty dress with the hem still intact.

Lupita shrugged. "I know. I usually clean up before going to bed, then throw dirt on my face before I leave the room. I keep it in a bag under the bed."

"No!" Mercedes couldn't believe it.

Lupita – the one everyone considered La Fea in the saloon – was actually one of the most beautiful, but she hid dirt under her bed so she could disguise herself otherwise.

"And you go to bed looking like this every night?"

"No," Lupita admitted. "I took extra care tonight because my father said I had to look nice for tomorrow."

Mercedes face fell. She knew what tomorrow was supposed to mean for the girl. How would her friend react when she knew the truth?

"Lupita, I'm sorry to have to tell you this, but your father is wrong. There won't be any wedding tomorrow."

"I don't know, Mercedes." A look of doubt crossed Lupita's face. "My father usually gets what he wants, and I'm afraid what he wants is for me to marry and get out of this town."

"It's not a bad thing – what he wants for you, Lupita. It's the way he's going about it." Mercedes stepped forward and took hold of her friend's hands. "You can't marry John, Lupita, because he's already married to me."

"Como?" Lupita took a step back. "How is that possible?"

"We found a priest and he married us."

A slow smile lit up Lupita's face. She threw her arms around her friend. "Ay, amiga. That's wonderful!"

"And that's not all." Mercedes hugged her back. "I made amends with God, too."

Lupita gasped. "So you finally bought the fairytale?"

"Oh, no, nena. This is no fairytale. If it was, then I could never have gotten away from this place."

"But you haven't gotten away from all this." Lupita's face grew serious. "If my father finds you here, you'll never get out again. Not alive anyway."

Mercedes grasped her friend's hands.

"I know, 'manita. That's why I need your help. I need to get the key to the gate."

"The key? But why?"

"To let John in so he can get his horse. That's the real reason we came here."

"For a horse?" Lupita rolled her eyes. "Are you serious?"

"Nena, you have no idea how serious." Mercedes cracked a smile. "I think he'd trade an arm or leg for the animal if he had to."

"Yeah, well, you're both going to trade a whole lot more than that if you don't hurry up and get out of here!"

"Then you'll help us?"

Lupita looked skeptical. Mercedes sent up a silent prayer that the girl would assist them.

"Alright." The girl conceded. "But if going against my father turns out bad for all of us, then I might be going with you!"

Mercedes wrapped the girl in a quick embrace.

"What are you talking about? You're going with us anyway."

The girl squealed with delight, then quickly covered her mouth.

"Are you serious?"

"Of course, I am! You didn't think I'd leave you behind, did you? You're like a sister to me."

"Ay, Meche!"

The girl threw her arms around Mercedes again, who warmed at the sweet moniker. They released each other and Lupita pulled on her arm.

"C'mon. I know where he keeps the key."

John quietly paced in the shadows behind Jericho. Where was Mercedes? What was taking her so long?

Maybe this hadn't been such a good idea after all. They could have done like Mercedes originally suggested. They could have married and just walked right across the street, into the good ol' United States, and been done with it. Then he could have found a job in one of the surrounding towns, maybe as a sheriff or something, saving up enough money until they could continue their travel back to North Carolina.

Nah, that wouldn't have worked either. The west was still a little too wild for John's liking. And this close to the border? Shoo, Belmonte could get a wild hair and decide to go after Mercedes. North Carolina was six whole states away, though. Seven if he counted the Arizona-Mexico border towns of Los Ambos Nogales. So the chances of him going after her were slim.

John stopped pacing and peered into the darkened courtyard. Maybe it was best to just shed this wretched disguise, get himself some troops, and return to storm the saloon. He dropped to one knee, bowing his head.

Dear, Lord. I don't know what's taking Mercedes so long, but I'm starting to get a bit antsy. Actually, I'm thinking that I might have to go on in there and get her out. But I sure don't want to do that if it's just gonna' make things worse. So, please direct my steps. Help me to know what to do.

The sound of dirt shuffling brought him to attention. John stood, wrapping the shawl over half his face.

"John?" Mercedes called out as she and Lupita approached the gate.

"Right here, darling." He met them at the bars. "You get the key?"

"We sure did." She fumbled with the lock, cranking the key until it clicked into place. "It was in Belmonte's room, in a small wooden box that he also keeps locked."

The hinges creaked as the gate swung open. John took his wife into his arms. He held her close.

"Then how did you get it out of the box?"

"I did that," Lupita spoke. "I took it back to my room and smashed it into a dozen pieces."

John chuckled.

"The two of you with a small army could probably raze this place."

The women exchanged looks.

"Hey, now." John warned them, a pointed finger directed at Mercedes. "Don't you go about getting any ideas now."

"You're right." She straightened her back. "We've still got a horse to save. Come on!"

The three of them raced along the back wall until reaching the corridor that led to the corral.

"Okay. Someone needs to stay out here and stand watch while I get Abby. So who's it gonna' be?"

"I will," Lupita volunteered. "If my father sees either of you, he's liable to shoot. Nothing will happen to me, though."

Despite her strong convictions, John thought the girl would be in more trouble than she admitted. Still, she had the best chance out of all of them.

"Alright, then. You stand outside and keep watch. Mercedes will stay in the middle so you can yell out any warning to her. Then she can pass it on over to me in the corral. Agreed?"

Their heads bobbed in agreement and John ran down the corridor, hand-in-hand with Mercedes. He released her when they reached the halfway mark.

"I'll be right back."

"Okay." She leaned in and gave him a quick kiss. "Hurry!"

"You better believe it." He reassured her, then ran down the corridor. It opened up to empty stables.

The sound of voices forced him to duck into one.

"You shouldn't mess with that horse, amigo. Remember what happened the last time?"

"That's not going to happen again." The sound of a gun clicked. "I'm getting on that horse one way or another."

"Ay, hue. We're supposed to be watching the horses – not riding them."

"Right. You do the watching and I'll do the riding."

John peered out from his hiding spot. One of the men ran off into the middle of the corral. Four horses, including Abigail, shied away from the man who made a beeline for the mare.

Maybe I can distract this one.

John quietly removed his gun from the holster. He pressed himself against one of the beams, hiding completely behind it. Then he kicked the dirt at his feet.

Sure enough, the Mexican turned around. He drew his gun and slowly walked toward the stall.

"Quién es?" He called out. "Come on. I know you're out there."

"It's just me!"

John's breath caught. What was Mercedes doing? Why had she left her spot?

"Qué haces aquí, Malinche?" The man walked past John's hiding place. "You're not welcomed here!"

"Neither are you," she told him as John jumped out from his spot.

The man turned just as John brought the butt of the gun down on his head. He collapsed to the ground.

John ignored the crumpled body at his feet.

"What are you doing here?" He demanded.

"Lupita said there are men in the courtyard. They're probably heading this way."

John looked around at the enclosed corral. It would be a bad place to get trapped.

A shot sounded from behind them.

"We've got to get out of here!"

He turned to find his mare still being chased, her pursuer filling the air with a string of expletives as he ran behind her.

John let out a high whistle. The horse immediately stopped and lifted her hind legs. The kick she gave sent the man flying backwards. He laid on the ground, motionless. John released another, lower whistle, and the horse trotted to him.

"Good girl, Abby." He patted her down. "That's a good girl."

"Do you think she can carry both of us?" Mercedes examined her leg. "She hasn't completely healed."

"We'll have to make due." He grabbed the horse's mane and hoisted himself up. Then he reached down for Mercedes. "Take my hand."

He pulled her up onto the horse, and she settled in behind him.

"Keep your head down!" He demanded as they raced through the corridor, the low ceiling mere inches above them.

They burst out into the empty courtyard.

"Where's Lupita?" Mercedes screeched.

John looked around, but saw no one.

"I don't know, but the gate is still open." John nudged the horse onward. He felt a pull on the back of his shirt.

"John, look!"

Mercedes pointed down to a small pool of blood on the ground, but said nothing more. She didn't need to. They both knew what had come to pass.

"There's nothing we can do for her now."

John echoed her sad thoughts. He clucked at the horse and she walked on, silence settling between them and Jericho.

Epilogue

Charlotte, North Carolina – Eight Months Later

"I don't think I can do any this." Mercedes gritted her teeth, beads of sweat dotting her forehead.

"Yes, you can!" Teresa encouraged her. "The baby's almost here."

"I see a head!" Catalina cried.

"Get the mirror," her mother instructed. "That way she can see all the great progress she's making."

Catalina did as she was told.

Mercedes looked down, then gave her a tired smile. She squeezed her eyes shut and bore down once more.

A small cry filled the room.

Teresa quickly cleaned the child.

"Look at your beautiful baby." She gushed and handed over the new bundle of joy.

A knock sounded at the door.

"Everything all right in there?" John's muffled voice sounded from the opposite side. "I heard a wee cry in there."

Catalina giggled.

"That man has near walked a hole into the floor. Every time I went out to get some more water, he was pacing so fast he'd almost bump into me. Matthew tried to take him outside for a walk, but he just wouldn't hear of it!"

Mercedes closed her eyes and let out an exhausted sigh. She grinned at the picture Catalina painted, easily imagining her worried husband outside.

He really is a good man.

Another knock sounded at the door.

"Ladies?"

Teresa laughed. "Let's not keep him waiting any longer."

Catalina rushed over to the door and pulled it open.

"She's ready to see you now."

John took his hat off and slowly crept into the room, Matthew following in behind him. The wood floor creaked under the sound of their boots. The baby stirred and John paused. He focused his sight on Mercedes.

"You alright, darling?"

"Hmmm." She hummed. "We both are."

"Yeah? Well, that's good." He crept a little closer. "So you decide yet on whatcha gonna' name him?"

"Him?" Mercedes giggled. "Better get ready for that shock, sir. This is the first of ten girls."

"It's a girl?" John whispered with excitement. He sat down beside the bed. "Bless the Lord, it is! Would you look at that?"

He beamed up at Matthew, then turned back to Mercedes.

"Do you want to hold her?" She offered the baby to him.

"I don't know. I'm a little afraid." John admitted. "She's so tiny and all… I wouldn't want to hurt her none."

"Don't worry. You won't." She held the baby out again, and he slowly wrapped his arms around her.

He ran one gentle finger down the child's cheek.

"Aw, she's even softer than a newborn colt. Prettier, too!"

Matthew laughed.

"Leave it to you, John, to compare a baby to a horse."

"Sure! I've got to train this youngin' early on. That way she'll be riding with the best of them."

"Riding with the best of them?" Mercedes laughed. "Are you going to teach her to shoot, too?"

"Yes, ma'am. I'll make sure this itty bitty gal knows how to take care of herself. Ain't no one coming around to mess with my little… Hey, what are we calling her anyway?"

"Lupita Maria."

John sobered up. He studied the baby for a moment, then gave her a small kiss on the cheek.

"Sounds like a right fine name to me."

He handed the baby back to Mercedes. She snuggled the sleeping child closer to her.

"We'll give y'all some privacy." Matthew wrapped an arm around his wife's shoulder, and they followed Teresa out.

Mercedes waited until the door shut.

"John?"

"What is it, darling?"

"Do you think we'll ever know what happened to her?"

He leaned over, taking both her and the baby in his arms.

"Honestly, I don't know." He said. "But I thank God for her and whatever she did to keep them away. We wouldn't have gotten out of there otherwise."

"I know." Mercedes swallowed hard, fighting back tears. "That's why I wanted to name the baby after her and Doña Maria. I'm so sad that they didn't make it to the border, but so thankful that they helped us get there."

"Don't be sad, darling." John kissed the top of her head. "We don't know the end of their stories yet. Something good might just come out of it. I mean, just look at us!"

Mercedes thought about what he said. Looking back on her journey, she knew he was right. Not only had she been saved from Jericho, but she had been saved from making the worst mistake of her life.

She looked down at the baby, and thanked God for such sweet redemption.

A Letter to Readers:

Thank you so much for picking up a copy of *Twice Redeemed*, the second book in The Jericho Resistance series. Everything you have read in this book is fictional. However, the premise of the story is based on a (largely forgotten) battle that occurred between Mexico and the United States of America during World War I.

The Battle of Ambos Nogales (Nogales, Arizona and Nogales, Sonora) took place during *three* wars – World War I, the Mexican Revolution, and the Border War, when a Mexican carpenter failed to stop at customs on his way home. A United States soldier shot at the man, who promptly fell to the ground. Customs officers on the opposite side thought one of their countrymen had been shot, and turned their guns on the American soldiers who returned fire and killed the officer.

Believing they were under attack, Mexican residents took up arms to defend themselves. However, they were eventually subdued when Buffalo Soldiers of the 10th Cavalry joined the fight, after securing heights and setting up a machine gun.

Due to the large number of casualties (including a Mexican mayor who attempted to surrender), both governments agreed that a divide should be created between the two nations. A chain linked fence created the first border wall.

Through research (books, internet searches, newspaper articles, and more) I was able to find many interesting little factoids regarding the history and people of Los Ambos Nogales. If you would like to know more, I encourage you to read the rest of the series, or connect with me online. Oftentimes, I look for people who would like to critique or review my books in exchange for advance reader copies. If you believe you would be interested in participating, then please visit me at:

www.mimimilan.com
http://tinyurl.com/h66r9r7
www.facebook.com/AuthorMimiMilan
www.twitter.com/thewritingMimi

For those of you who prefer snail mail, please write me at:

Mimi Milan
PO Box 19795
Charlotte, NC 28219-0795

Coming Soon

The Jericho Resistance | Book Three

The Fires of Faith

http://tinyurl.com/h66r9r7

A Taste of Mexico

Authentic Mexican recipes from the heart of Michoacán

Corn Tortillas

When I first moved to Mexico, a sister-in-law took me to the outside kitchen, saying she wanted to make me "a real woman." Of course, I was completely confused (and a little embarrassed) when I realized what she meant.

In Mexico, trucks pass by early in the mornings selling warm, tortillas *a la mano* for as little as ten pesos. However, there are no trucks passing by here in the United States (at least, not where I live). So I'm thankful my cuñada taught me how to make real corn tortillas.

Ingredients:

2 cups masa harina
1 ¼ to 1 ½ cups warm water
2 pieces of thick plastic (think freezer bags)
A wooden tortilla press

Instructions:

1. In a large bowl, combine the masa harina and water and stir. Knead the mixture until it forms a smooth, firm but moist dough. If it is too dry, add a little more water, 1 tablespoon at a time.
2. Divide the dough into twelve balls of equal size.

3. Line a piece of plastic on the bottom of the wooden tortilla press.
4. Lay one dough ball in the center. Cover it with the second piece of plastic.
5. Now, PRESS! Make it as thick (good for sopes) or thin (great for tacos) as you want.
6. Carefully peel off the dough and place it on a hot, ungreased comal (or griddle). Cook until he tortilla is dry and light brown, turning occasionally (takes about two minutes).
7. Place the tortilla in a warmer, or servilleta, until you're ready to it.

Frijoles a la Olla

I'm a bit of a mutt (Italian, Puerto Rican, German – the list goes on). So believe me when I say I've had my fair share of beans. Everything from red beans and rice to pasta faggiolo, beans have been a staple in our family for generations.

Know what?

The Mexicans got me beat.

Never in my life have I eaten as many beans as I did when I was in Mexico. I mean, it was served with almost every dish…

Every day!

Beans with queso fresco, rice and beans, refried beans on tortas… Whew! There were a lot of beans in that rancho.

So now you know. Any good Mexican meal should be served with a side of frijoles a la olla. There are many ways to make them, but here is my personal favorite.

Ingredients:

1 pound of pinto beans (or whichever you prefer)
1 ½ teaspoon salt
½ green bell pepper
½ red bell pepper
½ medium onion
1 garlic clove
1 jalapeño pepper (*if* you want a little heat)

Instructions:

1. Shift through the beans and remove any wrinkly old ones and rocks (yes, there are sometimes rocks in with the beans).
2. Put the beans in a strainer and rinse them well.
3. Toss the beans in a large pot and cover them with water (about two inches above the beans).
4. Bring the beans to a boil, then reduce to medium heat.
5. Add in the bell peppers and onion. By the way, these can be diced or sliced. Do whatever makes you happy. We like long, kind of thick slices in ours.
6. Squash the garlic so it breaks. Remove the skin and toss the whole garlic into the beans. Do not cut it up! The garlic is only meant for flavor. It is not to be eaten. (Right here is when you can add the chile peppers if you like it spicy.)
7. Sprinkle the salt on and give it a stir.
8. Allow the beans to cook until the skins break (usually about two hours in our house), stirring occasionally.
9. Top the beans with some queso fresco and cilantro. Serve with warm tortillas and a little Salsa Roja, if desired. Delish!

La Salsa Roja

This sauce is used on all kinds of stuff. Tacos, enchiladas… potato chips! If my husband can find a use for it, then best believe it's going in his stomach. Of course, that means you have to be able to take the heat!

Ingredients:

5 cups of reduced-sodium chicken broth
1 onion, cut in quarters
2 garlic cloves
12 dried New Mexico chile peppers (about 3 ounces),   with the seeds and stems removed, and cut into
        small, pieces (about an inch thick)
2 corn tortillas, torn into little pieces
Pinch of salt
Splash of Valentina (or whatever hot sauce you use)

Instructions:

1. In a large, heavy pot (kind of like a Dutch oven), combine the broth, onion, and garlic. Bring it all to a boil, then reduce to medium heat. Simmer for about fifteen minutes (uncovered).

2. Stir in the chile peppers and tortilla bits. Then remove it from the heat. Cover and let stand for about thirty minutes.

3. Blend the mixture in a food processor. Then strain it. (You may have to do this in more than one batch, depending on the size of your blender). Return all of it to the pot.

4. Bring it to a boil again. Reduce the heat and simmer it (again, uncovered) until it thickens (about another fifteen minutes).

Refried Beans

Guess what? Mexicans do not typically eat refried beans. Seriously. In the three years that I lived in Mexico, I <u>never</u> had them as a side dish, on a taco, etc. However, I did get them on tortas. In fact, that's the only way I ever ate any refried beans in Mexico. So I give this super-duper easy recipe to you. Otherwise, you won't be able to make the delicious torta!

Ingredients:

2 tablespoons of vegetable oil or pork drippings
Half the pot of frijoles a la olla

Instructions:

1. Heat the oil in a skillet. Place the beans in the skillet.
2. Heat the beans over medium-high heat until it begins to boil.
3. Reduce the heat. Simmer while using a large metal serving spoon (or potato masher) to flatten the beans.
4. Enjoy!

Torta

Perhaps one of the best things that I've eaten in Mexico (and my husband would agree), is a torta. Now there's many different meats a person can use. My husband likes the milanesa de pollo (breaded chicken), as well as the ham. Personally, I'll take either/or. Sometimes I even like it with just the veggies!

Ingredients:

Bolillo
Refried beans
Lettuce
Tomato
Avocado slices
Queso fresco

Instructions:

1. Cut the bolillo in half (lengthwise).
2. Slather on the refried beans. Line them with your choice of meat.
3. Add the slices of tomato, followed by slices of avocado. Add the lettuce.
4. Sprinkle a little bit of queso fresco if you so desire.
5. Slather the other side with more refried beans (or a little mayo, if you prefer).

6. Heat the torta on a griddle (kind of like a panini) until warm and golden brown on each side, lightly pressing it until flattened.
7. Serve with a side of jalapeños de vinagre (or spread on a bit of the salsa roja).

Enjoy!

Huevos y Frijoles

John and Mercedes share a meal in *Twice Redeemed* when she and Doña Maria whip up a traditional Mexican dinner. Actually, it's a meal that took me completely by surprise when I first went to Mexico and was introduced to it. Huevos y Frijoloes (Eggs and Beans) is a dish served in el rancho most days of the week, because of the ease of making it (not to mention the affordability). In fact, it is so simple and delicious that our family continues to make the meal although we're once again stateside. It is *that* good. Even my "chicken nuggets and hamburger" kids love it!

Ingredients:

3 eggs, beaten
3 cups Frijoles a la Olla
1 Tablespoon Vegetable Oil
Hand Masher

Instructions:

1. Heat the vegetable oil in a pan.
2. Pour in the beaten eggs and cook them the same as you would scrambled eggs (until dry and fluffy).
3. Add the beans (fijoles a la olla) and cook on medium heat for about five minutes. Turn the heat down to a low simmer.

4. Mash the eggs and beans with the hand/ potato masher while they continue to simmer.
5. Serve piping hot with warm corn tortillas.

Optional:

Want to get really authentic? Add a few slices of avocado to your bowl of beans. Top with the salsa roja and a little queso fresco on top for a little something extra.

Mexican Corn Cake

When I was younger, my mom would make what she called "Mexican corn cake." While indeed a mouthful of cheesy goodness with a small spicy kick, it wasn't actually *Mexican* corn cake at all. More like Southwestern cornbread or something.

See, Mexicans love chiles. However, they don't necessarily put them in EVERYTHING. One thing that I never had while living in Mexico was spicy bread *anything*. I'm not saying it didn't exist in all of Mexico. It just wasn't to be found in el rancho of Santa Rosa. Between that small ranch and the surrounding pueblos of Casablanca and Maravatío, any type of bread I ever ate was sweet.

So in memory of early morning walks to the neighborhood tienda where pan could be bought for a peso a piece, I present to you this little bit of sweetness.

Ingredients:

1 Tablespoon softened butter
An additional ½ cup of softened butter
3 cups of sweet corn kernels
1 14-ounce can of sweetened condensed milk
½ cup sugar
4 eggs (room temperature)
1 cup of all-purpose flour
2 teaspoons of baking powder

½ teaspoon of salt
Canela (cinnamon)
Honey

Instructions:

1. Preheat the oven to 350° after making sure the rack is set in the middle. Grease a square baking dish (about two quarts large) with the tablespoon of butter. Set that aside.
2. Combine the corn and sweetened condensed milk together in a blender until the kernels are chopped up fairly well. Then set it aside.
3. In a large mixing bowl, beat the ½ cup of butter and sugar with an electric mixer on medium speed until the mixture becomes light and fluffy. (About two minutes.)
4. Add the eggs, one at a time, beating them until mixed. Beat in the corn mixture. Then set it aside.
5. In a smaller bowl, add the dry ingredients (flour, baking powder, and salt). Add this flour mixture to the wet ingredients, beating it until it is just combined.
6. Pour the batter into the greased baking dish. Bake it for approximately 45 minutes, or until a wooden toothpick comes out clean when inserted into the middle of the cake.
7. Cool the cake on a wooden rack.

Optional:

Now for the yummy part! This dish can be served in one of two ways.

Desayuno (Breakfast) – Enjoy a slice of this delicious Mexican corn cake with a nice cup of Mexican hot chocolate, or café con leche.

Postre (Dessert) – A slice of this delicious cake can be warmed up and topped with a scoop of your favorite ice cream. My favorite is vanilla. Of course, my husband prefers dulce de leche. Both are delicious with a drizzle of honey on top, and a little sprinkle of cinnamon. Go really crazy and add some whipped cream!

BEST. DESSERT. EVER.

Holy Mole

Baptisms. Weddings. Quinceañeras.

Every single Mexican fiesta I've had the pleasure of attending have always had one common menu item.

Mole.

A spicy sweet sauce found at the heart of Mexican soul food, mole is generously offered with boiled chicken and red rice. So don't mind serving a little extra to your guests. After all, that's what tortillas were made for. To sop up all that holy mole.

Ingredients:

1 Tablespoon of butter
3 minced garlic cloves
1 Tablespoon of Mexican chili powder
¼ teaspoon of ground canela
3 Tablespoons of cornmeal
3 cups of chicken broth
        (from the chicken you boiled, of course)
3 Tablespoons of nut butter (like almond butter)
2 ounces of chopped semi-sweet chocolate
        (you can use the bittersweet chocolate if you're looking to cut back on sugar)
A dash of salt

Instructions:

1. Heat the butter over medium heat in a medium-sized saucepan. Add the garlic and sauté it until just browned (maybe a minute).
2. Stir in the chili powder, cinnamon, and cornmeal.
3. Whisk in the chicken broth. Bring it to a boil.
4. Reduce the heat and whisk in both the nut butter and chocolate.
5. Simmer the mixture for about ten minutes. Then add salt to taste.

Serve over the boiled chicken with rice, beans, and tortillas on the side. A true delight!

Chocolate Atole

This is my absolute all-time favorite drink ever! Early Sunday mornings, when the sun was cradled on the horizon of a fiery sky, I would run out to the street and greet a lady from the neighboring pueblo. She pushed a wheelbarrow with two large ollas, both filled with delicious aromas that tantalized the senses when she lifted their lids. One was filled with tamales (a few special ones without jalapenos sat on top just for me). The other was filled with the most amazing chocolate drink I had ever tasted.

Atole.

Made with the same masa used for tortillas, atole is an age-old, hot Mexican beverage. It's usually served on cold mornings or special occasions. So I was very fortunate to live in an area where a woman earned her living by delivering it to neighbors. I begged the woman to tell me her recipe. Thankfully, she agreed. Now, with a little bit of love and labor, I can enjoy this delicious wonder here in the states.

Ingredients:

½ cup of masa harina
    (flour that you use to make the tortillas)
3 cups of warm water
    (a little more may be needed)
1 cup of milk
4 ounces of semi-sweet chocolate

(I just use ½ a tablet of Abuelita)
½ teaspoon of canela (or 1 cinnamon stick)
   (if you're not using the Abuelita)
Pinch of salt
1 teaspoon vanilla extract (or 1 vanilla bean)
Optional: 1 small Piloncillo cone
   (for those who want it really sweet)

Instructions:

1. Place the masa in a large olla. Add the warm water 1 cup at a time while constantly whisking. (This is important so you don't get clumps.) Set this aside on the other eye of the stove.
2. In a small pot on the stove, add the milk and chocolate on low heat (as well as the piloncillo cone if you want it extra sweet). Stir until the chocolate dissolves. Add this mixture to the masa, and simmer on low to medium heat – stirring often.
3. Add the salt, canela, and vanilla bean. Continue to cook the atole until it thickens. This should take about ten minutes.
4. Remove the canela and vanilla bean (if those are what you used instead of ground cinnamon and vanilla extract).

Serve this with a little plain Mexican corn cake and you've got yourself some of the best Mexican comfort food imaginable.
   Buen provecho!